Cover Model

By

Marie Rochelle

This is a work of fiction. Names, characters, places, and incidents are products of the author's imagination or are used fictitiously and are not to be construed as real. Any resemblance to actual events, locales, organizations, or persons, living or dead, is entirely coincidental.

Red Rose™ Publishing
Publishing with a touch of Class! ™
The symbol of the Red Rose and Red Rose is a trademark of Red Rose™ Publishing

Cover Model by Marie Rochelle

Red Rose™ Publishing
Copyright© 2007 Marie Rochelle
ISBN: 978-1-60435-905-3
ISBN: 1-60435-905-6
Cover Artist: Rae Monet
Editor: Red Rose™ Publishing

All rights reserved. No part of this book may be used or reproduced All rights reserved. No part of this book may be used or reproduced electronically or in print without written permission, except in the case of brief quotations embodied in reviews. Due to copyright laws you cannot trade, sell or give any ebooks away.
This is a work of fiction. All references to real places, people, or events are coincidental, and if not coincidental, are used fictitiously. All trademarks, service marks, registered trademarks, and registered service marks are the property of their respective owners and are used herein for identification purposes only.

Red Rose™ Publishing
www.redrosepublishing.com
Forestport, NY 13338

Thank you for purchasing a book from Red Rose™Publishing where publishing
comes with a touch of Class!

Chapter One

He slowly slipped the sleek dress from her shoulders. It slid down her warm smooth body, flowing down into a satiny pool of black material around her feet. He let his eyes slowly inch their way over her body, loving how the dark red bra and matching panties stood out against her rich dark toffee skin.

The cursor on the screen blinked back at her as if daring her to write another word. "Why can't I write anything?" Kissa "Bri" Collins complained pushing herself away from her computer desk. After having writer's block for the past two weeks, she thought maybe it was over by now, and decided to try another shot at her latest romance book; but it just wasn't happening for her.

She had even gotten so fed up with the computer, she had tried to write the book out by hand, something she hadn't done in over a year. That idea didn't help her out either.

"I'm never going to make my deadline if I don't clear my head and focus on my characters," she sighed getting up from the desk.

Kissa left the room and made her way towards the kitchen in the back of her new house. She moved in here six months ago and couldn't be happier. With its fenced in backyard, underground pool and flower garden. It was the perfect spot for a writer like herself to relax and unwind any time of day of the week.

Once in the kitchen, she grabbed an apple out of the bowl on the kitchen table and took a bite. She'd rather eat a huge slice of the chocolate cake that she had in the refrigerator, but was too early in the day to be eating something sweet, and she wouldn't be able to stop at one slice. Resting her backside against the counter top, she replayed the conversation she had with her agent over in her head. Africa kept telling her that if she got out more, then she would be able to finish her new book without a problem, but she didn't think that was the case.

Africa Abbott, her agent, was the kind of woman who drew attraction every time she walked into a room. She was the life of the party and never seemed to have a bad day. On the other hand, she liked being alone with her thoughts and feelings, and Kissa knew that's what made her fans take pleasure in her writing.

Kissa had been writing romance novels for the past three years, and the last three of her four books ended up on the New York Bestsellers list. However, she doubted this new book she was working on would. It was driving her up the wall and she was about to delete the entire story from the computer and start over from scratch.

Why couldn't she connect with these characters as she'd done in the past? She loved the plot of the story when she thought of it last month, but now it just wasn't working for her.

Her previous books kept her fingers glued to the keyboard because hero and heroine seemed to jump off the computer screen at her. She usually wasn't able to type fast enough to keep up with them and their ever changing plot twists. Yet, with this book, she wasn't losing any sleep because she felt the need to finish this book.

"What am I going to do?" Kissa muttered, worried about her career. This was the first time she had ever had a problem finishing a book. Africa was so impressed how she could finish a novel in less than six months, but something was preventing her from connecting with these new characters.

Kissa continued to munch on the apple as she left the kitchen and headed outside for a breath of fresh air. Maybe the balmy June sun would help clear her head and get her writing juices flowing.

"You look horrible. Have you been getting enough sleep?" Africa drilled her. "I don't need my best friend and my favorite client getting sick on me."

Kissa yawned then shook her head. "No, I've slept just fine. This new book is driving me up the wall. I've been wondering why I can't seem to connect to the characters. I believe it's the hero. As much as I try, I'm not able to put a face with his name. How can I write about a hot guy and make my readers fall in love with him if I don't have a clue what he looks like?"

"I think I might have some good news for you," Africa grinned, making her toffee eyes shine even more.

Any time Africa got excited about something, it always meant bad news for her. "What is this good news you have for me?" she asked. "Will it benefit you or me?"

"How could you ask me something like that?" Africa retorted. "When have I ever done anything that wasn't helpful to you?"

"You don't remember when you sent me to that nudist camp, so I could have better descriptions of the human body," Kissa hissed. "I almost died when that man came up to me naked as the day he was born."

She saw Africa trying not to laugh and it pissed her off even more.

"I've never been so thankful to be a black woman in my entire life. Lord, I know my face turned a thousand shades of red."

"But the man never knew because you have that wonderful, flawless russet skin," Africa stated waving an ebony hand towards her face. "Anyway, if I'm not mistaken, your description of the naked male body was perfect in your last book. So, I guess in the end I didn't do anything wrong," Africa gloated.

"Don't get too cocky," Kissa stressed. "If I haven't wanted to stay for the entire day at the nudist's camp, I wouldn't have."

"Yet, you did and Naked became you third bestseller," Africa cut in. "Now stop complaining and listen to the wonderful idea I pitched to your publisher. I know you're going to love it."

"I won't be so sure if I was you." Kissa hated when Africa came up with these crazy ideas for her books. Yes, It helped the novels sell.. But damn it, why did she always have to be the one who was the guinea pig?

"I suggested that you should be at the open call for your cover model for you latest book. You weren't at the last three and I don't think that was right. Since you have proven you can sell books, I thought you might like a hand at picking out the male model."

Kissa couldn't believe her ears. "Are you serious?" She had wanted to be a part of the open call for the past couple of years, but she could never fit it into her schedule.

"These lips aren't lying to you," Africa smirked. "The publisher is having the model search here in Dallas and I thought you might like seeing all those mouth-watering men walking around."

"You know how much I hate it when you get all full of yourself," she complained at her agent. If Africa wasn't such a good friend to her, she wouldn't be able to put up with her sometimes.

"I'm good and you know it."

Kissa hated to agree but she couldn't help it. "Fine, you did a good job this time. I have to admit, I didn't think your surprise would be this amazing."

"Great, so I'll let the publisher know that you'll be at the open call. I think they're trying to get it from two weeks from now."

"Give me the information when you get it and I'll be there," Kissa exclaimed and she really hoped that Africa wasn't setting her up for something totally different.

Chapter Two

"You're the perfect man for the job. She'll never suspect you."

"I'm not standing there in a pair of jeans and no shirt while some strange woman ogles my body," Forbes Huntington snapped. "I've worked too hard to get here for that kind of shit. Why don't you do it?"

"I don't look like you and I'm too old. Shit, none of the guys in the Bureau can go undercover with this assignment," Zane Rogets, his boss, complained.

Forbes brushed a lock of his sun-streaked dark brown hair away from his slate eyes. At thirty-eight he didn't want to waste a month of his life going undercover.

"What about Leo? He looks like Antonio Sabato Jr. She'll love him. He's not bad-looking guy. Send him and not me. I don't want to go," Forbes uttered.

Zane strolled further into his office closing the door behind him. "Leo is already on a plane for Canada for another assignment, so that just leave you, buddy." He smirked taking a seat.

"Tell me again why this is a good idea?"

Leaning forward in the black leather chair, Zane pinned him with a hard glare. "We have been trying to catch Thomas

Collins for the past eight years, but he never stays in one place long enough."

"We got word that he's going to Dallas and the Bureau wants someone in place before he gets there. Thomas is very intelligent and won't take to strangers coming up to him. If you do this, then we'll already have you there and he won't think twice about it."

He was irked by Zane's cool, aloof manner. Forbes was going to be the one stripping down showing what he had to a room full of people. There had to be a better way to go about this.

"Isn't there a Plan B?"

"We all like Plan A and we're going to stick with it. You're making too much of it. She's an attractive woman, you shouldn't have any problem attracting her attention. I bet she'll drool over you the same way other women do."

He hated when Zane tossed his success with women in his face. He couldn't help it that both of his parents were former models and he got good genes. The people that hung around him focused on his looks more than he did.

"I'm not going to be able to get out of this, am I?" Forbes asked but he already knew the answer.

Zane shook his head. "Sorry. So, you better get ready. You need to get yourself together because you're leaving in the next couple of days," Zane ripped out the words impatiently.

"How long do you want me to stay?" Forbes' voice was calm; his gaze steady as he returned Zane's look.

"Stay until you get the case solved. I want Kissa Collins to become your main focus. Do anything and everything you have to make sure land the cover of that book. Ms. Collins is the only way we're going to get close to her uncle." Zane got up and left the room without waiting for a response from him.

Forbes tossed out a string of curses before he finally calmed down. Picking up the phone, he booked the next available flight to Dallas. He only hoped that he was the kind of cover model that Kissa Collins was looking for.

Chapter Three

Sitting behind the table, Kissa eyes traveled over the twelve men standing in front of her. She tried to disguise her annoyance so they wouldn't see how frustrated she was with them. She found herself inexplicably dissatisfied that none of them fit the image of her hero, Brad Wagner.

Her pulse wasn't leaping in her throat, she wasn't dreaming of being crushed against their wide chests. Kissa was by no means impressed by the models that she and the publishers finally decided on. Her publishing company said because of a deadline that she had to pick twelve guys, however, she was beginning to think it was an enormous mistake to decide on any of them.

"How many of you know who I am? Have any of you ever read any of my books or held one in your hands?"

Kissa waited for what seemed like hours while the guys exchanged glances with each other, but not one of them opened their mouths to answer any of her questions. How could she put any of them on her upcoming cover? It would be an insult to her hero. She needed a man that would grab a woman's attention from the aisle.

Have her counting the hours until she came home from work and cuddle up with him on the couch. What woman didn't want to get lost in the pages of a sizzling novel after a long, hard day at work? However, these men wouldn't make a thirsty woman drink from the pages if they were filled with water.

When Africa suggested this to her, she had been on cloud nine. Now she felt like she had wasted a week of her life. "Guys, I'm sorry but I'm not gong to be able to use any of you after all," she apologized. "I want to thank you for you time."

"What's the problem?" One of models chimed in. "I've been on covers of romance novels before and readers have loved me."

Kissa stared at the guy who had just spoken. Sure, he probably had sold millions of books with his Roman good looks; nevertheless, he wasn't what she was looking for.

"Shawn, I don't doubt that you have," Kissa stated, "but you aren't quite what I'm looking for to sell my latest novel. I'm not saying I won't use any of you in the future. I'm only saying that you aren't the guy I need for this particular book."

"Okay, but keep my photo and call me if you change your mind," Shawn replied, then left the room with the other eleven guys following behind him.

The sound of Shawn's voice stayed in her head long after he and the other guys were gone. Was he right? Was he the guy she was looking for and she just wasn't aware of it? Could he fit every woman's fantasy? This was her first time being involved with picking out a male cover model for her book and Shawn had been both her publisher's and Africa's favorite of the twelve.

Yet a part of her knew there had to be another guy out there who would be her hero..

"Africa is going to be infuriated that I let the guys go, but I couldn't see any of them as Brad. If I didn't feel him, I wouldn't be able to make my readers feel him either."

Kissa gathered all the head shots together and pushed them into a pile at the end of her table as a light pounding start at the side of her temple. "Great, after the long day I've had now, I'm going to top it off with a headache," she groaned. Taking a deep breath to calm her nerves, Kissa closed her eyes and zoned everything else out while she massaged her temples, wishing her headache would go away.

The sound of the door opening and closing to the studio broke her concentration, but she was too worn out to open her eyes to see who it was. If she had to make a guess, it was probably Africa coming to check on her. Her best friend did that a lot, as if she didn't think she had to ability to take care of herself.

Sure, she worked way too hard and missed sleep when it came to her writing, but she wasn't crazy enough to make herself sick. "Africa, you didn't need to check on me I'm fine."

"I don't know who Africa is," a voice, deep and sensual answered sending a ripple of awareness through her.

Shocked at hearing a masculine voice, Kissa dropped her hands and her eyes flew open. She merely stared, tongue-tied, at the unbelievable man making the large room look smaller with his presence.

The rich outline of his muscles strained against the fabric of his white t-shirt. He was tall, handsome, with an amazing proportioned body that made her mouth dry. His compelling gray eyes, the perfect features, the confident way he had his shoulders back made Kissa wish he was here for the job of her cover model, but she wouldn't get that lucky.

His five o'clock shadow gave him even more of a manly appearance and the way his lips were firm and sensual at the same time made her wonder all sort of things that she shouldn't. Even his dark brown hair that was streaked with highlights from the sun made his naturally tanned complexion smoking hot. He had a ruggedness that attracted her.

"I'm sorry. Can I help you?" Kissa asked coming out of her daze.

"Yes, I'm looking for Kissa Collins. I'm here about the cover model call," the man said. "I hope I'm not too late. I was supposed to be here last week but something happened and I couldn't make it."

Damn her luck!

"I'm sorry but you did miss them. I've already chosen the twelve."

Chapter Four

Zane told him to come here and make Kissa Collins his main focus and that wouldn't be a hard thing to do. She was absolutely mesmerizing. He was almost at a loss for words when she raised her head and looked up at him.

Her face was a perfect oval and her smooth mahogany skin glowed inviting his fingers to test its silkiness. The corners of her mouth turned upwards more than they turned down. It was almost like she never frowned, but was always happy. Kissa's dark hair was pulled back with a few wispy bangs fell to fall across her forehead.

The v-neck of her red t-shirt made her throat looked enticing and showed off her firm high perky breasts. He wouldn't be able to tell anything else about her until she stood up from behind the table.

Zane had sent him here to stay close to Kissa, and after seeing her, Forbes knew he wasn't going to have a problem with that. He only problem might be focusing on her too much and not putting enough time towards the case.

"Are you sure there isn't anything I can't do to become a part of the top twelve? I've traveled a very long way to get here," Forbes explained. "I always thought of thirteen as being my lucky number."

"What is your name?" Kissa asked moving from behind the desk.

Forbes lost his train of thought after Kissa moved from behind her table. Her body was sinful and he wanted to sample it every way that he could. She had nice hips and shapely thighs, the kind he loved holding on to while he made love to a woman. Kissa had the body of a fifties pin up model. Everything was in the right place for a man to love and his cock swelled to attention at the possibility of being with her.

"Forbes Huntington," he uttered honestly before he could give her his alias. What was wrong with him? He had never done that in his entire fifteen year career.

"Move back a little, so I can get a better look at you." Kissa waved her hand in his direction.

Stepping back, Forbes stood still while Kissa came closer and circled his body, the soft aroma of her perfume and closeness of her body made his cock swell even more in the confides of his jeans.

"Mr. Huntington, I've to be honest with you. I got rid of the other models because I wasn't happy with them."

"Does this mean I might have a chance?"

Kissa stopped by his left arm and ran her fingers over his muscles. "You do fit the hero in my book better than the other guys did," she confessed removing her hand.

"Do you have a head shot that I can take to my agent and the publishers," she asked, standing back in front of him. "I think you're the perfect guy for my next book, but I have to get their approval too."

"No, I don't have any photos," Forbes answered.

"May I ask why not? How did you think you would get hired without a head shoot?"

Here comes my cover, Forbes thought. "One of my friends told me about your open call. He wasn't interested so I decided to take a shot at it."

"I'm very impressed with you and your looks. Mr. Huntington. You're everything that I'm looking for in the cover model for my book."

Stepping closer until not an inch separated him from Kissa, Forbes let his eyes slowly travel the curvy contours of her luscious body. "That's good to hear. When do I get a chance to prove I'm the right man for you?" He thought that Kissa's form was built better than a Coke bottle; not a thing was out of place.

Licking her lips, Kissa tossed her head back. "You don't have to prove a thing to me. I'm already satisfied with what I see," she flirted back.

He had to stop before things got out of hand. Kissa was a distraction that he wasn't planning on and he had to control his attraction to her or his job would be over before it started.

Forbes stepped back a safe distance from her. It was better for him to be safe than sorry. "Does that mean I have the job?"

"No, I only get half of the vote. Africa and my publisher have the final say. So, if you can leave me your name and number, I'll set up a meeting and get back to you." Kissa went around the desk and gathered up the photos.

Taking a card of back pocket, Forbes tossed it on the desk to Kissa. He had a couple of them made up before he left home. "You can reach me at that number. It's my cell phone and I usually have it on during the day."

"You have a business card, but not a head shot," Kissa said, picking up the card off the desk waving back at him. "Don't you find that a little strange?"

"No. My friend has a new printing business and made me some card up for free. He was testing out his new printer and wanted something to print. I liked the white and black together. Plus, I think the cards are a lot easier to carry around."

Forbes couldn't believe how easily he was telling Kissa his usually story. He had told this story so many times he could do it with his eyes closed.

"I'll let everyone know about you and how impressed I was by you, Mr. Huntington," Kissa stated, "then I'll give you a call. It should be longer than a week."

"I'll be waiting for your call," he gave Kissa a quick wink and then left the room.

Outside Forbes flipped open his cell phone and punched three on his speed dial; it rang a several times before Zane finally answered in his usual gruff tone.

"How did it go?"

"I met her and she's double gorgeous. Why didn't you tell me how she looked?"

"Forbes, you aren't there to pick up a girlfriend," Zane snapped. "The Bureau sent you there to catch her uncle. Now tell me how it went?"

"She has to set up a meeting with her publisher and another woman, but I'm not worried."

"Are you sure? We can't get overly confident."

"I'm positive that I landed the job and Kissa is attracted to me, so getting on her good side shouldn't be a problem."

"It better not be. We can't lose any more money chasing Thomas Collins across country. Dallas will be his last stop," Zane retorted. "Don't call me. I'll call you," with that said his boss ended the call.

Forbes snapped his phone shut and then made his way to his rental car that was hid in the very back of the alley. Once he got inside he waited until Kissa finally made her way out of the building. She came out the door and he thought she even looked better in the daylight. He watched as she made two phone calls before she hurried over to her car parked across the street and drove off.

"I need to get a trace placed on that number so I know who she's talking to. I hope it takes her uncle a while to show up because I want to get Kissa a lot better than I know her right now," Forbes muttered then started his car.

Chapter Five

Brad couldn't get over how Dru didn't know how her seductive body and the curve of her hips had him rock hard the second she walked into his office. The black dress she was wearing made her legs longer and slimmer. All he could think about was stripping her out of her clothing and making love to her in front of his desk.

Dropping his hand underneath the desk he unzipped his pants and stroked his cock, imaging it was Dru's hand. The contrast of her darker skin against the whiteness of his was turning him on even more. She was across the room organizing his files without a clue he was about to erupt in the palm of his hand.

A few more strokes were all he needed and he would finally be rid of the pressure building up in his body. Brad bit down on his lip to keep from screaming out loud. He could feel it was about to happen.

"Mr. Wagner, do you need a hand with anything else?" Dru's smoky voice asked as she came closer to his desk.

Hitting the save button, Kissa fell back into the chair happier than she had been in a long time; her writing was coming easier to her now. As if she was on a roll. She hadn't been this motivated in weeks.

"I might actually finish this book by the deadline," she muttered. "I don't know what happened to me but whatever it is I don't want it to go away."

Stop lying. You know what has gotten you into the writing mood.

Forbes Huntington.

Yesterday when she had called and told Africa that she had gotten rid of the twelve models, the sound of her screaming had echoed in her head most of the day. Kissa remembered she had to talk Africa back down for a good half an hour.

Africa wasn't about to let her off the hook until she promised that Forbes was the man she was looking for. She still found it hard to believe that a guy with his good looks didn't have a portfolio.

There should be a law against the way his muscles stretched out that white t-shirt; it took all of her will power not to ask him to remove it. Not only was Forbes blessed with a downright too-good-to-be-true body, but his face was perfect. Lord, a woman could get lost in those double thick black lashes.

"Stop lusting after a man that might be working with you after today," she scolded herself. "Keep him at arm's length and everything should be just fine."

The sound of Amerie's Take Control chimed from her cell phone and she quickly checked the phone number before answering. "Didn't I tell you that Forbes was one the hottest guy that I've ever laid my eyes on?"

"Where in the hell did you find him?"

"I told you he just walked in off the street after I let the other guys go. I almost thought he wasn't real. Isn't he perfect for Brad Wagner?" Kissa gushed. "I almost told him that he had the job on the spot."

"Bri, you've impressed the publishers with Forbes. He had them eating out of his hands."

"I can't believe you still call me by that silly nickname," Kissa laughed. She had gained the nickname Bri back in college. One of her friends said that her laid back personality reminded her of a cool breeze on a warm summer day. She had made the mistake of telling Africa about it and now her agent used it any chance she got.

"I think it's so cute."

"You would," Kissa sighed. "When do I get to attend Forbes first photo shoot?"

"Tomorrow," her agent replied. "I'm not sure about the location, but when I have all the details, I'll call you back."

"Sounds good to me," she answered.

"Bri, you really did good picking out Forbes. I think he'll make your book another best seller. Call you later."

"Okay." Kissa ended the call and tossed the phone back on her desk. She had never wanted twenty four hours to pass as quickly as she did today.

* * * *

"Any sign of the uncle yet?"

"No, I just came back from meeting with Kissa's publishers and they loved me. I start taking pictures tomorrow and she'll be there, so I'll start hinting around about her family," Forbes explained. "I don't want to seem too interested. It might tip her off."

"Do you think she's involved?" Zane asked his interest piqued. "As far as I know, Thomas Collins has always worked alone."

"I can't say for sure, but I'll be able to tell you more about that after I spend time with her tomorrow," he bragged. The anticipation of seeing Kissa again made his palms sweaty.

"I'll do my best," he assured his boss. "I'll go by the book until the end."

"You better," Zane threatened before the dial tone rung his ear.

Tossing his phone on the table, Forbes strolled around his hotel room and his mind wandered about Kissa Collins. After talking with her agent today, he knew that Kissa was single and had been for quite a while. Africa told him that Kissa focused on her writing so much that she seldom made time for a man in her life.

He didn't think that Africa even realized how much information she was giving him. He just said a few things here and there and Africa opened up with him. Despite the fact that she told him so much about Kissa, he could tell that Africa loved her.

The thought had entered his mind to bring Kissa's uncle up, but he decided against it at the last minute. He had to lay low, and asking questions about Kissa's family would have made her agent suspicious.

Tomorrow he was going to start the first day of his photo shoot for the cover of Kissa's new book. He couldn't wait until he saw her again. The soft lure of her voice was so calming to his nerves. It had been a long time since a woman attracted him with just the sound of her voice.

Usually he had all these different qualifications that a woman had to fit first before he thought about taking her to bed. As an F.B.I. agent, he had to be very careful about who he slept with. Several of the guys at the Bureau had girlfriend after girlfriend, but he wasn't like that. He believed in committed relationships.

He wanted a woman who was interested in doing things with him when he wasn't working and had the time to spend with her.   A huge part of him was very affectionate when it came to the woman in his life. Hugging and kissing her, holding her hand and showing her daily how much she meant to him. Running his fingers through his thick hair, Forbes couldn't forget how good Kissa felt next to him yesterday. Her slim fingers as they brushed over his muscles caused an erection faster than he had during his college days, and back then he was always standing at attention.

"Zane would kill me if he knew I gave Kissa my real name." Forbes still couldn't understand how he let that happen. During his long career as an agent he had run into good-looking women before and kept in character. What was it about Kissa that he hadn't given her the alias Zane came up with?

"Hopefully, I can get through this assignment without him finding out about my attraction to Kissa and it will fade as quickly as it started," Forbes uttered.

Chapter Six

Brad held his breath as Dru kept coming closer and closer to his desk. She only had to move a few more feet and she would get an eye full.

He quickly removed his hand and stuffed his stiff cock back into his pants. Brad didn't know how Dru might react at seeing him long and hard in the middle of the day alone with him in his office.

"No, I'm fine Dru," he replied in a calm voice that shocked him. "Why don't you take an early lunch? I have a handle on things around here."

"Are you sure? I can always grab something and come back earlier if you really need help."

Brad clenched his hand underneath his desk at the thought of Dru coming after he had his way with her. No, he had to get rid of her and fast.

"Yes, I'm positive," he groaned as a bead of sweat popped out on his forehead. God, she was killing him, standing there in that black dress. Why couldn't she just leave and let him finish getting off in peace?

"Ohmigod. Mr. Wagner, are you okay?" Dru asked rushing over to his side, she grabbed a few tissues off the box on his desk and wiped the sweat off his forehead "There is something wrong with you. I've never seen you sweat like this before."

Keep rubbing me like that and you'll see more than sweat, sweetheart, Brad thought as he tried not to stroke himself again. Dru was driving him crazy with her full breast pressed against his arm and the slow movements of her hand.

"Dru, stop touching me," he snapped grabbing the tissues out of her hand. He flung them down on his desk and tried to ignore the growing erection in his pants.

"Fine, I was only trying to help you," Dru hissed then stopped in mid-sentence.

Brad wondered what had gotten Dru to finally stop touching him. He noticed the look on her face and then followed the direction of her eyes. His erection wasn't inside in pants as he had first thought but stick out begging for attention.

"Dru, I'm so sorry," Brad apologized as he hurriedly tried to fix the problem. There was no way Dru wasn't going to their supervisor and report him. He would unemployed by the end of the day.

"No, don't," Dru whispered brushing his hand away. "I want to see you."

Kissa re-read the paragraphs again making sure it had the sensual desire that she was trying to achieve with this story.

Brad was confident, along with being a well-known playboy, but he loses all of his confident around Dru.

He wants her more than any of woman that he had ever met, but Dru constantly looks past him as if he is made of ice. She wanted the office scene to hint that there could be a little more between them than either one of were willing to admit.

"Oh, I can't wait until I start on the rest of it tonight," she gushed saving the new chapter to her computer. "Africa is going to be so impressed with me." Kissa's eyes searched the screen. She was looking for a way to make the scene hotter and as she thought of one, the ringing of the phone made it disappear from her mind.

"This better be good. You might me lost my train of thought," she growled into the phone.

"We have a problem," Africa's panicked voice practically screamed over the phone.

"What did Forbes not show up for the photo shoot?" she asked turning off her computer. She prayed that her sixth sense was taking a lunch break when she met Forbes.

Kissa made it to the location of the photo shoot for her cover in less than twenty minutes and it usually took her forty minutes or long. "Africa, why are you in such a panic?" She flung out the question as she hurried over to her friend standing by a rack of clothes underneath a nearby tree.

Taking off her sunglasses, Kissa tossed them into her oversized purse. She loved how the perfect Texas sun beamed down on her bare arms, making her fall in love with her hometown more than she already was; she couldn't ever think about leaving this place. Anytime she wanted to she could take her laptop out to her sun porch and spend the day working out there from sun up to sun down.

"The female model is running late," Africa moaned drawing her attention back to the discussion at hand. "Her agent called me and said Valerie's plane was held over for security reasons. She might not even make it for another four hours."

"WHAT!!??" Kissa screamed. "You can't be serious." This wasn't happening to her. "What am I going to do? I finally found the perfect guy and no one is going to see him on my cover."

"Hmmm...that isn't true," Africa hedged. "I did have you rush down here for another reason."

She wondered what was running through the creative mind of her agent. Africa's off the wall ideas regularly had her guessing what her friend would think of next.

"Why do you look like you know something that I don't?"

"Don't freak out when I tell you this," Africa said, taking a step closer to her. "I truly think it's a wonderful idea, but you may not think so."

Kissa held her ground. She didn't take a step back from Africa, however she watched her agent warily because she wasn't breaking eye contact with her. It was something big that Africa was excited about.

"I promise I wouldn't freak out," Kissa stated depicting an ease she didn't necessarily feel. She became more uncomfortable by the minute as Africa's silence continued.

"Remember, you promise."

"Are you going to tell me or not?" Every fiber in her body warned her that she wasn't going to like what Africa going to tell her.

"The photographer wants you to replace the female model." The words rushed from Africa's mouth and then she took two quick steps back.

"HAVE YOU LOST YOUR MIND?" Kissa shrieked.

Chapter Seven

Forbes flinched at the sounds of feminine screams coming from outside his trailer. Dropping his shirt on the floor, he charged out the door in total F.B.I. mode and raced down the steps towards the screams. As he rounded the corner, he stopped dead in his tracks. Kissa was standing there arguing with her agent.

Her sienna skin sparkled in the dark green sundress that hugged her body as if she had been poured into it. Coffee hair with soft light brown highlights was brushed back off her head into a shot ponytail that ended at the nape of her neck. His attraction the sensual young author was all wrong; it wouldn't lead anywhere, not with him here to arrest her uncle, but he couldn't help how his body responded around her.

Kissa was good-looking plus ten. She had such a passion that he found most women were lacking nowadays. She was a career woman on a mission and that alone made her hotter.

"Man, you have to stop or Zane will kill you." Forbes got his body under control and went to see could he calm down Kissa.

"Bri, it won't be as bad as you think. You've seen Ian's work before and loved it," Africa argued with her "Why don't you think he can do the same job for you?"

"I'm not a model and I have never wanted to be one. I have my dream job. I get to write books. I don't want to be on the cover on them. Hell, I don't want an author photo and bio on the back flap."

"Ladies, what seems to be the problem?"

Not now. I can't deal with him with Africa bugging me about this.

"Forbes, thank you for your concern, but we have it under control," she replied spinning around to face the man she couldn't stop dreaming about. Kissa couldn't have stopped her mouth from falling open if someone had paid her.

Tight black shorts cupped the most intimate part of Forbes and the rest of his tight, toned, amazingly tanned body was bare. The same confident gray eyes she loved the first time she laid eyes on him stared down at her with interest and hint of something else.

"I heard the two of you all the way in my trailer. I'm not sure if you've things under control or not," Forbes countered. "Why don't you tell me what it was about? Maybe I can help you out."

"The female model we wanted isn't going to be able to do it, so Ian wanted Kissa to stand in, but she's scared," Africa answered before she could.

"I'm not scared," Kissa denied shooting her agent a hard look. "I'm just not a model."

"I've to disagree there," Forbes said with a shake of his head. "You skin is perfect and those midnight eyes of yours could make anyone fall in love with you."

She chewed on her lower lip and tossed her head back taking a long look at Forbes. "You don't have to flirt with me. You already have the cover."

"Sugar, I'm not flirting with you," he corrected. "I'm giving you a compliment. The way I would flirt with you is on a sexier level than this and you wouldn't forget it."

Kissa gasped as the heat in Forbes unexpected words made her heart race. As she paused to catch her breath, she started to see this photo shoot in a different light. It might be a lot of fun to have her body pressed against Forbes' in scorching pictures.

"Alright, I'll do it," she agreed secretly counting the minutes until she got to touch Forbes' naked body. "Where do I go and change?"

"There's a trailer next to Forbes," Africa answered. "I'm pretty sure he wouldn't mind showing you the way there."

"She's right. I would love to show you where to get undressed. Do you need help with that dress?"

Kissa could flirt with the best of them so Forbes Huntington better watch out. "I'll let you know after we get there."

Taking her by the arm, Forbes lead her away from a grinning Africa and she wondered who had really won the argument after all. "How long have you been here?"

"A little less than an hour," Forbes replied glancing down at her. "I was trying on different shorts when I heard you."

Everything that made her a woman warned her against falling for him, but Forbes was a man to be ignored. "Lucky shorts," she whispered under her breath missing the look at Forbes gave her.

Kissa was so lost in her own thoughts that she didn't realize that Forbes had pulled her between the two trailers before it was too late. Her body was trapped between one trailer and Forbes's body. His bare chest was burning a hole through the thin fabric of her sundress and it felt out of this world.

"What are you doing?"

"I think we should get to know each other better," Forbes answered tilting her chin up with his hand.

Okay, she was game for this little game he was playing. "Why?"

"The photographer is looking for a hot steamy cover and we can't give him one if we're uncomfortable with each other," he replied pulling her closer to him. "I think we need to practice."

"Practice," Kissa mused. "Practice what?"

"This," Forbes growled before his mouth covered hers.

Warning spasms erupted within her, however, Kissa pushed them down and wrapped her arms around Forbes wide shoulders, and allowed herself to get lost in the kiss.

Forbes' lips were moist and firm, as they demanded a response from her. His mouth continued to explore the fullness of her mouth until she opened it allowing his tongue to slip inside. The first touch of his tongue sent shivers of pleasure racing through her.

Standing on tiptoes, she deepened the sensual assault even more with her own tongue, shocked by her eagerness with a man that she barely knew, but wanted with everything that she had in her. She was burning up for Forbes and even the light summer breeze wasn't cooling her off.

Leaving her mouth wanting more, Forbes' mouth left hers and trailed a path of light kisses down her neck and her shoulder until they stopped at her breasts. Grabbing the sides of her dress, Forbes gave it a firm tug and her breasts sprung free. She knew she should tell him to stop, but she had wanted this since she laid eyes on him.

"Darling, you're so beautiful," Forbes groaned before he licked a nipple and then drew it into his waiting mouth.

"Oh," Kissa moaned sliding her hands through Forbes thick hair. "We shouldn't be doing this." She was trying her best to see reason. They weren't that far from the crew, anyone could pass by and see them.

"Why not?" His lips brushed against her swollen nipple as he spoke. "Are you afraid someone might see us?" Forbes asked shoving her dress up to her waist, his eyes dropped down past her waist and he cursed. "Shit, you aren't wearing any underwear. Are you trying to make me take you right here?"

"It's hard to even wear a thong with this dress," Kissa hissed as Forbes slipped one long finger inside of her wetness. "It's so snug."

"I think you didn't wear any panties to taunt me," he accused adding another thick finger. "Were you going to let me have a little peek at your kitty cat?" Grabbing her leg, Forbes wrapped it around his waist drawing his finger even deeper into her drenched body.

"No, I wasn't going to do that," Kissa panted as she tried not to scream out loud. Forbes was increasing the pace of his fingers and it was getting harder for her not to yell at the top of her lungs.

A light sweat was covering her body from Forbes and his magical touch along with the ninety degree sun beaming down on their bodies. Kissa had never been so turned on in her life. It was like a scene out of her romance books. The undeniable sexy hunk and his woman got so lost in each other that they couldn't wait until they found a room.

"Do you want to tell me what you were going to do then?" Forbes inquired easing his fingers out of her body until she only felt the tips at her entrance.

"I don't know. I hadn't thought that far," she confessed squirming on his hand. "Please don't stop."

Forbes removed his hand from her throbbing body. He licked and sucked at her nipples until they were pebble hard. "I wish I could but I can't," he apologized as he quickly fixed her dress.

"Why not?" she practically hissed.

"I hear someone headed this away and I'm a jealous man. I don't want them to see how breathtaking you look right before your orgasms hit you."

"Orgasms," Kissa whispered. "You make it sound like I was going to have more than one with you. I haven't been with a man yet that is that good in bed."

"Kissa, if we didn't have this photo shoot, I would show you that I'm not a boastful man. I could have you screaming at the top of your lungs."

Brushing her hands over her dress, Kissa fixed it better than Forbes had it, and winked at him. "Promises that will go unfilled," she taunted moving around the trailer before Forbes could make a grab for her.

Chapter Eight

Her hand kept inching closer and closer to his erection. The thought of Dru's hand wrapped as his cock almost had him coming before it was time. No! He couldn't let this happen. His first time he enjoyed the pleasure of her fingers on him wouldn't be a quickie in his office.

He wanted them to be in a huge empty bed with all the sheets flung to the floor, so he could explore every inch of her delectable body. This wasn't the time or the place for what he wanted to do.

"Dru don't." Brad's hand shot out preventing Dru from touching him. "We can't do this here."

"You don't want me to touch you?"

Hell yeah! He wanted her hands all over every inch of his body just not a work. Anyone could walk in and see them and despite how much the idea turned him on. He wasn't going to put Dru through that.

"No…I don't want you to touch me."

Shaking off his grip Dru stepped back from him so quickly that she almost stumbled. "Oh," she whispered in a shaky voice. "I'm sorry I got the wrong idea. Maybe I wasn't supposed to catch you with your pants down."

Hearing the hurt in Dru's voice Brad hurriedly fixed his clothing and stood up. "I want you to listen to me."

He couldn't let her think that he didn't want her. That was so far from the truth.

"Hey, it was an honest mistake. I guess." She shrugged moving back even more until she was only inches from his closed office door. "How about we put this incident behind us? I can pretend it never happen if you can."

"I don't want you leaving like this. Stay and hear me out. You aren't seeing the whole picture."

"Brad, I wished that I could but I'm going to be late for my lunch date. I've to leave." Dru spun around and went out his office door before he could stop her.

"Is that the famous book I keep hearing so much about?" Forbes fell into to the next to her bringing along that natural sexiness she loved so much.

Kissa hit a couple of keys on the computer and save her latest chapter. She couldn't afford to lose it after it had taken her so long to find her muse. "I thought you would still be working on that last photo shot."

"I still can't believe Carmen showed five minutes before we were going to start. I really wanted to see you in that little red two-piece bikini." Forbes' gaze raked up and down her body.

"I don't know what Ian was thinking," Kissa replied pretending her body wasn't on fire from the salacious looks Forbes was tossing her way. "He should have known better."

"Ian is a photographer. He appreciates a beautiful woman when he sees one."

"Are you flirting with me?"

"What if I am? What are you going to do about it?"

Leaning across the table Kissa got directly in Forbes's perfect face. Damn, if he was this good-looking she wondered what his parents looked like. "I might have to tell you to stop. I don't fool around with the people I work with."

Forbes brushed his thumb over her bottom lip making the sexual chemistry between them even hotter. "If we didn't fool around earlier what do you call it, Miss Collins?"

"A bad lapse in judgment," she answered removing Forbes' hand away from her mouth.

"I have to disagree with you. I think it was something neither of us had experienced before and I want to try it again. Your kisses are like a bag of potato chips…I just can't have just one."

Giggling Kissa fell back against her seat brushing away tears. "Please tell me you haven't tried the line on other unsuspecting women."

"I thought it was funny. It made you laugh."

"I guess it did." Kissa agreed getting lost in the soothing sound of Forbes' voice.

"I find you fascinating. Go out on a date with me."

The smile instantly vanished from Kissa's face as she gathered up her belongings and stood swiftly. "I'm sorry. I can't do that. Now if you'll excuse me." With those words uttered she went towards Africa's trailer without a backward glance at Forbes.

"How are things going on your end? Have you gotten Kissa to open up to you yet?"

Moving the curtain back in place, Forbes left the window and paced through the sitting area that Zane was resting in. He couldn't keep doing this to Kissa. His feelings for her were growing stronger with each passing moment.

"Can't we find another way to get Thomas Collins?"

"No, this is the best way and from what I've seen, you're doing a wonderful job."

"You're watching me?" he snapped, stopping in tracks by the man who had been his best friend for years. "Do you not trust me to get the job done?"

"It's not that," Zane stalled. "It just seems like you aren't pushing Kissa hard enough. She's either always working on this book or with her agent. You need to cement yourself in her life until her uncle shows up."

"You do know that I'm only doing this because I'm ordered to," Forbes informed his boss. "Kissa is an amazing woman and I don't want to hurt her. Let me tell her the real reason I'm here."

"Absolutely not!" Zane yelled, jumping from the couch so fast that he almost hit his leg on the table. "We can't…no, you can't afford to leave now. You're too far in this and beside what would Kissa think?"

"She would be hurt if I disappear without any warning. And the last thing I want to do is have Kissa upset with me."

"Glad to hear it," Zane stated patting him on the shoulder then strode towards the door. "I need to go, but don't forget I can check in anytime. So don't get too comfortable being with Miss Collins." With those parting words, he opened the door and then closed it softly behind him.

"That's easy for you to demand since you aren't the one falling in love with her." Forbes dropped into the seat Zane left empty. "Am I willing to risk my career for a woman that I barely know?"

The most difficult part of his job was the isolation. Sometimes for weeks, even months at a time, he would work primarily by himself without a partner and it didn't bother him, because it came with the job. For as long as he could remember, becoming an F.B.I. agent had been a long life dream of his.

Becoming a F.B.I. agent hadn't been easy since he had to meet stringent physical requirements along with holding a bachelor's degree in several different areas. Language and Diversified were the two hardest things for him. Law, Science and Accounting turned to be out a lot easier than he thought they would.

For years he found the solitude of his job rewarding until he laid eyes on Kissa Collins; everything changed for him then. He started to wonder could she handle the long periods of time he would be away from her. His career was exciting, constantly filled with travel for long period of times.

In addition, the F.B.I. performed a background check; They checked to see if he had a criminal record, interviewed friends and associates. They had even questioned past landlords as well as roommates as far back as his early college days.

All the investigation had lead to drug tests and later, a polygraph test. Once he passed all of that, he was sent to the F.B.I. Academy in Quantico, Virginia. There he studied firearms, self-defense, how to investigate a crime scene, and many other law enforcement techniques.

The usual retirement age of most agents was after twenty years of service, some retired in their late fifties. He was fast approaching his twenty year mark in the Bureau and before Kissa, leaving the F.B.I. seemed impossible. Now it didn't look so bad.

"How can I keep the woman I'm beginning to care for and the job I love?" It was a hard question with an even harder answer. Forbes wasn't ready to lose either one, but having them both seemed impossible. When all of his secrets came out after this assignation, he was going to lose one and he didn't have a doubt in his mind it would be Kissa.

Could he quit his job for her and become a teacher, attorney or private investigator as most of the other agents did after they left? No, none of those jobs fit him. He would be bored within a year's time.

"Why am I even thinking about all of this?" He questioned standing up stretching. "I know that Kissa is attracted to me but that doesn't mean she wants a relationship. I'm not even sure she doesn't already have a boyfriend." His blood boiled at the thought of another man being with the woman he wanted.

"Get a grip, Huntington, or you're going to blow your cover. I need a break from all of this." Searching the room for his keys, Forbes snatched them up and left his hotel room.

Chapter Nine

"I want two scoops of vanilla and add some sprinkles on top of it too." Kissa dug inside the bottom of her purse while she waited for her ice cream. As she found the correct money the strangest sensation came over her body.

"You should have told me that you liked liking vanilla. I would have offered up my body in a hot second," a warm male voice whispered by her ear.

Shivering at the picture of Forbes lying naked on his back while she licked her way down his well-defined body almost made Kissa drop the money in her hand. Taking a deep breath, she bullied her body back under control and faced the wicked man behind her.

The forest green t-shirt was plastered to his perfectly portioned body and shoved into a pair of tight jeans that molded his hard thighs and everything else in between. Kissa slowly ran her tongue over her bottom lip, not knowing what the action did to Forbes' semi-aroused body.

"Shame on you," she scolded. "You shouldn't offer me things like that. I might take you seriously."

Forbes backed her so fast into the corner by the ice cream booth that she didn't have time to blink. "You might have forgotten what we did at Ian's photo shoot, but I haven't. Do you know how many dreams I've about you at night? In some states, they are illegal."

"That isn't my fault," Kissa answered over her racing heart. "We had a moment of passion and nothing else. I told you I don't sleep with the men I work with."

"Technically, I work for my model agency and your publisher until the cover is finished. We can date and have all the fun we want," he whispered tracing the swell of her breasts with his finger. "Don't you want to have fun with me? It's summer which means passion is in the air."

"Stop," she moaned trying to move her body away from Forbes. His erection was poking against her, causing a pool of moisture to rush between her legs. "We can't be doing this in public."

"Would you rather we do this in private?" Hard fingers pulled at her nipples while his tongue licked at the side of her neck. "You smell delicious. Does the rest of you smell this good?"

"Ma'am, your order is ready," a cheerful young voice piped from around the corner cutting into her rendezvous with Forbes.

Embarrassment flooded her face and she was thankful for her darker skin so Forbes couldn't see it. "Let go of me." She shoved at his hard chest, but he wouldn't move out of her way.

The wind stirred around them gently and Forbes' cologne hit her senses. The powerful scent stirred a deep longing within her body and mind. Her experience with men wasn't that extensive, but she sensed that Forbes Huntington was trouble with a capital "T".

"Will you wait for me while I order my ice cream? Or will you run away the second my back is turned?"

"I'm not a coward. I'll wait for you other there on the bench in the park," Kissa stated as she stared at Forbes' wide shoulders. *Girl, what are you getting yourself into with this man?* She wasn't sure of the answer to that question, but she was willing to learn more about Forbes to find out.

"I believe you," Forbes replied moving away from her.

"Thanks." Kissa hurried around the specimen of the perfect man and quickly paid for her ice cream. "Don't stand me up," she tossed back as she went in the direction of the bench.

"Don't worry, darling. I never leave a pretty woman waiting for me," Forbes' playful voice yelled behind her.

"Tell me about your family. Are the only child? Or do you have a large family?" Forbes already knew the answers, but he had to test Kissa and see how honest she was.

Swallowing the last of the ice cream in her luscious mouth, she wiped the corner of it with a napkin, then tossed it into the trash can next to her. Sunlight shined on her black hair making it shimmer. She was wearing another sundress like the one at the photo shot, only this one was a salmon color that highlighted the deep rich brown tones of her skin.

The need to reach across and trace her smooth skin had him stretching his arms across the back of the bench. At the very last minute he chose to sit across from Kissa on another bench instead of next to her. It was getting more difficult to resist the yearning to make love to the temptress seated across from him.

"I had an older brother, but he died in an accident while he was at college. Trey was pledging to a fraternity and something went wrong. One of the hazing stunts went wrong; unfortunately his body wasn't found until the next day by his roommate."

"I'm so sorry. How old were you when he died?"

"I was a freshman in high school and I don't think my parents ever got over it."

"Are you parents still alive?"

Kissa swatted at a bee buzzing by her ear then continued. "No, they died my senior year of college in a boating accident."

"You've been on your own for a while now. Haven't you?"

"I'm not alone. I've my Uncle Thomas. He's my mother's brother and after I graduated college, he invited me to move here and I stayed with him for about a year."

Forbes schooled his features hoping that Kissa wouldn't see the exhilaration in his features at her mentioning her uncle's name. This is what he had been waiting for these past two weeks. "Is your uncle the one that got you interested in becoming a writer?"

"Yes, he is. He read one of my papers I wrote in college and told me I should get paid for my talent."

"So you took his advice and the rest is history?"

"You can say that. My uncle is the coolest. My brother and I always had the best presents from him when we were little. My uncle never seemed to be able to hold down a job, yet he had the best of everything."

"I bet he did," Forbes mumbled under his breath.

"Did you say something?" Kissa asked.

"No, I was just thinking out loud," he lied.

"Care to share?"

"I was thinking about how soon I would get another chance to kiss you again. Don't tell me you haven't been wondering the same thing." Forbes held Kissa's eyes with his until she squirmed on the bench seat.

"This won't work between us. You'll be gone after this job is over. I don't think it would be for the best for us to get involved."

His radar went on red alert. Was Kissa was blowing him off because there was another man in her life and bed? Could he be falling hard for someone that already possessed an emotional attachment to another guy?

"Do you have a boyfriend and is that why you're blowing me off?"

Chapter Ten

"Forbes, I'm not blowing you off. I've told you the reason why we can't get involved." Kissa wanted Forbes with an intensity that she never thought she could feel, but it wasn't the right time for her to get in a relationship.

"Flimsy excuses and you know it," he countered leaving his bench to come sit next to her. "You want the same thing I do and I'm not backing down until I win you over."

"Forbes, you're a gorgeous man..."

"Thank you," he grinned jumping in. "I think you are a very stunning woman."

"You didn't let me finish," she sighed. "What we are feeling is a burning attraction to each other. It might fade out after a couple of dates."

"Have you always been this scared of men or I'm the only man that brings out this fear in you?"

"I've told you earlier that I'm not a coward."

"Prove it," Forbes taunted.

"How do you want me to prove it?" Kissa questioned.

"Spend some time with me."

One perfect eyebrow arched over a chocolate eye. "I'm with you now, aren't I?"

"You know what I mean. I want a real date. Do something that doesn't involve your book."

"You aren't going to drop this, are you?" She already knew what Forbes' answer would be, but she had to ask anyway.

A sinful smile hovered at the corner of his firm and attractive mouth. "No...now invite me over for dinner."

"Is dinner all you want?" Kissa asked skeptical of Forbes' hidden agenda.

"For now yes, but it might change tonight once I get you in my arms," he answered with a wink.

Kissa made a clicking sound with her tongue then shook her head. "You're a confident man, Mr. Huntington. How do you know that I'll even end up in your arms tonight?"

"I'm a smart man. I can sense the battle you're having right now with your conscience. So there's no doubt it my mind you'll end up pressed against my chest tonight with my lips against yours."

"Stop it." She moaned at the aphrodisiac vision Forbes' words made materialize in her mind. "You can't be doing this to me. I'm on a deadline. I have to finish my book and get ready for a promotional signing for my bestseller that's out now."

"Live a little. Don't let Kissa become a work alcoholic. I know you're a wild woman waiting to happen; all you need is the right coach to bring her out of you."

53

"Are you that coach?" she asked facing the handsome man next to her.

"You bet your ass I am. I love spontaneity and it's even hotter when it comes from a woman."

Did Forbes think he was fooling her? The only thing he wanted was an invitation to her house, so he could try seducing her with that mesmerizing voice of his. Hell...what was she thinking? He already had her wondering about how their bodies would fit together when they made love.

Don't think...just do it.

For once in your life do something that doesn't fit into your perfect little box. A man like Forbes doesn't drop into your life but once in a lifetime. He's attracted to you and you're attracted to him, so why not act on those feelings? Making up her mind, Kissa swallowed down her insecurity and jumped in with both feet.

"I usually eat around six o'clock," Kissa told Forbes. "Do you think you can be on time?"

"This will be a real date?" Forbes asked without the usual playfulness to his voice. "No talking about work at all. Can you deal with that?" A challenge was tossed into the air.

Moving her mouth until it was within kissing distance of his, Kissa whispered, "Yes I can manage that. But my question to you is can you handle me?" Heat flared suddenly in Forbes' gray eyes the second before his talented mouth captured hers.

Swiping his tongue along the seam of Kissa's lips, Forbes tried to gain access to the sweet treat inside. The small hint of vanilla ice cream that still lingered on her full mouth brought a growl from deep within his chest. He never thought kissing a woman after eating ice cream could be so erotic.

He cupped the back of Kissa's head, tilting it back for a better angle of that plump bottom lip he loved so much. His tongue wasn't a second away from entering her moist haven when the chiming of his cell phone broke the spell.

"What's that?" Kissa whispered leaning back her voice raspy with unleashed passion.

"Cell phone," he growled snatching it from his pocket.

"Speak!"

"Agent Huntington, stop making out with Miss Collins in the middle of the park. You aren't here for that," Zane ordered in his ear.

"How in the hell do you know what I'm doing?" Forbes eyes roamed over the park until they landed on the black Lexus in the parking lot off in the distance.

"I'm your boss. It's my job to know your whereabouts. Now, take your hands off of her before I make you remember the real reason you're here." The click of the phone completed Zane's final threat and made him extremely nervous.

"I have to go." He stood up and then pulled Kissa next to him. "But I'll be at your house tonight for dinner. Do I need to bring anything?" Forbes' chest swelled at the desire that still lingered in Kissa's beautiful eyes as she looked up at him.

"No, I can take care of everything. I only want you to bring this amazing body of yours." Trailing her fingers down the middle of his chest, Kissa stood on her tiptoe and kissed him on the side of his mouth.

"See you later," she murmured then slipped away before he could deepen the kiss.

Forbes waited until Kissa was completely out of sight before racing over to Zane's car and jumping inside. "What in the hell do you think you're doing here? Spying on me?"

Zane snatched off his sunglasses and flung them on the dashboard. "I was saving your ass. You can't get involved with Kissa Collins. She's our only link to her uncle and you're about to ruin that for us."

"I'm not ruining a damn thing. She's invited me over for dinner at her house tonight. Hopefully, I'll get a chance to look around and find out some information."

"Are you sure Kissa isn't on to you?"

Forbes thought about how she always exploded in his arms any time the two of them came together. No, she may be a bestselling romance writer, however she couldn't fake passion like that. She was on the same page as him. She couldn't wait to rip his clothes off and make love in the handiest place that they could find.

"No...she isn't on to me."

"Wonderful," Zane said pinning him with cool dark brown eyes. "Make sure you keep it that away. I don't have the money to hunt down Thomas Collins again."

Zane was always about business and nothing else. He wondered has his overly demanding boss even been in love. "Have you ever been in love? I can't recall the last time I heard you talk about going on a date. Your life can't be wrapped around the Bureau twenty-four seven."

"I don't discuss my personal life outside the office and you know that Forbes." Picking up his sunglasses, Zane shoved them back on his face. "Besides I'm not here to talk about me. I'm here to make sure you do your job."

"It will be done. Don't worry about it."

"You better be telling me the truth or it's both of our asses on the line."

Chapter Eleven

"I feel a little undressed," Forbes complained as he walked into the neat yet comfortable house. The door closed softly behind then Kissa appeared next to him looking breathtaking in an off-the-shoulder scarlet dress.

"Don't. I think you look very handsome," Kissa complimented as she stood in front of her date. The jeans Forbes wore molded his long powerful thighs making her very envious of them. The gray dress shirt underneath a suit jacket drew her attention to his muscular arms. "What you're wearing is perfect. I have our meal set up out by the pool."

"I brought something for you," he purred moving closer.

"I don't see anything in your hands. Is it in your pocket?"

"No."

"Hmmm...is it in your jacket?"

Forbes gave his head a small shake and the ends of his air brushed his collar. "Wrong again." Cupping her chin in the palm of his hand, he leaned her head back and gazed down into her eyes. "Do you want to guess again?"

Kissa ran the tip of her tongue across her bottom lip, pleased with the way Forbes' eyes followed the light caress. "I'm not having any luck so how about you just tell me."

"It would be my pleasure little Miss Romance Writer," he breathed on her lips the second before his mouth ensnared hers in a long, slow wet kiss.

She put her arms around his neck and pressed her body against his until not an inch separated them. His hands roamed her back as his moist, firm mouth demanded a response.

Cool wind from the air conditioner brushed her thighs as one large hand moved her dress and skimmed over her hips and thighs. Kissa didn't want to stop, but she had to before things got out of hand.

"Forbes, we have to stop. Our food is getting cold," she breathed lightly between parted lips.

"Let it get cold. We can warm it up later," Forbes answered picking her up and carrying over to the couch. He laid her down gently and covered her with his hardness. "I can't wait anymore to make love to you. Please let me love you."

Everything about this was wrong, but her heart wasn't listening. Her body was reacting to having him this close and honestly she didn't want to stop. "We haven't known each other that long. Don't you think this is a little sudden?" she asked grasping for straws.

"I know you feel this burning attraction between us," Forbes challenged kissing the side of her neck. "It started the second our eyes connected at the opening call you had and hasn't stopped since."

"Are you always so confident?"

"Yes. Does it bother you?"

The light sensation of his tongue dragging across the swell of her breasts made her nipples rock hard. Grabbing the hunk above her trembling body, Kissa pulled Forbes' mouth back down to hers. She wasn't going to think about tomorrow. This was her romantic moment and she was going to live in it. She kissed him with a hunger that she had kept hidden from other men.

Raising his mouth from her, he gazed into her eyes. "Are you telling me yes?"

"Yes, I want to make love to you," Kissa replied trailing her fingertips over his wide shoulders. "I can't wait until I see this magnificent body naked."

"I hate to keep a beautiful woman waiting," Forbes said standing up pulling her with him then swung her into his arms. "Which way to your bedroom?"

Kissa wrapped her arms around Forbes' neck and snuggled closer. "Straight down the hallway, the first door on the right."

"I'm glad it's close. I don't how much longer I could wait to make love to you." Hurrying down the hallway, Forbes pushed open her bedroom door and strolled in, kicking it shut behind him. He kept walking to the bed and deposited her in the center.

"You look so damn sizzling in this dress that I hate to take it off," Forbes said removing his jacket. He tossed it in a chair across the room and quickly undid the buttons of his shirt. Leaving it hanging open, he dropped a knee down on the bed while shoving her dress up past her thighs.

"I've to say you look pretty good yourself, Mr. Huntington." Kissa leaned back on her elbows raking her eyes of the toned bare flesh in front of her. "How about you take off the rest of those clothes? I want to see all of you."

"Only if you take off yours," Forbes countered moving back off the bed.

"Deal," she grinned kneeling in the middle of the bed. Kissa placed her hands at the bottom of her dress. "You go first."

Forbes' powerful well-muscled body moved with ease as he stripped out of his remaining clothes tossing them into a nearby chair. She had seen him half-naked before tonight. His shoulders looked a yard wide with skin the color of molten bronze. She also noticed there weren't any white lines on his body which meant his tanned in the nude.

Sandy hair lightly covered his legs and arms making her mouth water for the chance to touch him and learn their texture. Finally her eyes moved to the part she wanted the most and she wasn't disappointed. Forbes' erection stood proudly from his body, waiting for her.

"Do you like what you see? Would I make it into one of your romance novels?" his aroused voice questioned, making her wandering look snap back up to his eyes.

"Your ass is so fine, I would have a sequel to your story. There's no way I could do you justice in one book."

"How about you just remove that dress for starters and you can think about putting me in a book later?"

"Oh...I better get this off. I can't have you thinking I'm not a woman of my word," Kissa teased. In the next second the dress was over her head and on the floor.

Forbes thanked God he didn't have heart problem because the sight of Kissa's perky breasts, smooth stomach and barely there g-string would have done in him. Her perfect mocha skin contrasted wonderfully to the ruby red underwear and belly chain. He never figured her the type of a body piercing, which turned him on even more.

"I can't find the words to describe how good you look tonight," he whispered tracing the chain with his index finger. "Did you do this to tempt the hell out of my sanity?"

"Is it working?" Her dark eyes were beautiful as satin as she stared up at him.

"More than you'll ever know, my little writer," he confessed giving the underwear a firm tug baring her lower body to him. "I can't wait to show you how much I appreciate the extra step you went for me." Forbes gently laid Kissa back on the bed and pressed his mouth against the side of her neck.

Chapter Twelve

"You're so beautiful," Forbes whispered removing his mouth from her neck cradling both breasts in his hands. "When I first saw these I had the hardest time taking my eyes away."

He bent his head and ran his tongue across one tip. "I could kiss and suckle them all night long."

"Why don't you?" Kissa suggested arching her back giving him better access to her chocolate treats.

"I don't mind if I do," he growled latching onto Kissa's left breast. Forbes went back and forth sampling the goodies the hot woman beneath him had to offer him. He had never tasted anything this sweet until now. The need to keep sucking and tasting clawed at him until Kissa's body tightened and the first orgasm hit her.

"You're amazing," Forbes praised kissing her swollen lips. "I've never made a woman come just loving her breasts."

"That was a first for me too," she confessed running her hands down his sweat covered back. "I had no clue my body could do that. So you're pretty amazing yourself."

"Let's see what other first we can share together." His fingers trailed down the center of Kissa's drenched body until they came to rest between her thighs. Parting her damp curls with his thumb, Forbes played with the swollen nub he found hidden there.

Purring in the back of the back of her throat, Kissa spread her legs even wider, giving him better access to slip two fingers inside. They were instantly gripped tighter, making his cock swell even more with the need to possess the goddess beneath him.

"Damn baby, you're so tight," he growled pushing his digits further inside until he was knuckle deep. "Has it been a long time since you been with a man?" Forbes wanted it to have been a while. Kissa wouldn't be comparing him to any other man tonight or ever if he had anything to do with it. She was his from now until forever.

The emotions he felt for Kissa ran deep and he wasn't about to lose her for the world. Not to another man or anything else that may arise after all of this was over.

"Please...stop talking," she panted, breasts heaving with every breath she took. "I'm only thinking about you and only you."

"Not a good enough answer." He removed his fingers and kneeled between Kissa's warm thighs. "Tell me." Forbes pushed then ran his tongue across her wet entrance. The sweet taste of her essence coated his lips and tongue, driving him to do it again.

"Oh, my God!," her screams ricochet off the walls as he lapped up the juices that kept pouring from her body. "Forbes, please don't stop," Kissa begged as he cupped her tight ass in his hands pressed his mouth as close as it could get. He was there when her second orgasm hit her and he made sure one drop wasn't wasted.

Quickly moving away from Kissa's spent body, Forbes found his discarded pants on the floor and unwrapped the condom, covering his painfully hard erection. Getting back on the bed, he repositioned himself and entered her with one long thrust. He almost blacked out at the sheer pleasure it felt to finally be inside of her. It was better than all of the dreams that came to him late at night in his hotel room.

"Kissa, hell baby you're so damn wet and snug. You're a man's wet dream come true and you're all mine," he panted withdrawing only to thrust back in again at a slower pace. Forbes didn't know when he'll have the chance to make love to Kissa again before his assignment was over, so he wanted this to last forever.

"Forbes, this feels so good,' Kissa moaned arching her back as her hands pulled at the sheets beneath them.

"Do you want it to feel even better?" Forbes asked as an idea suddenly popped into his head.

Deep brown eyes stared into his as he measured the tempo of his thrusts. "Can you make it better?"

"Let's see." Kneeling in the middle of the bed, he wrapped a pair of toned smooth brown legs around his waist and placed

Kissa's hands underneath the headboard, bending her body just a little to get better depth.

"Hold on," he whispered then began to move slowly and little by little built up to a speed that had both of them screaming for the ultimate release.

Kissa never knew it could feel this good when it came to making love. The last guy she was with only wanted to get his pleasure. After that was achieved, he was out of the bed and in the shower.

The slow pressure of desire that Forbes was making her feel was more arousal than anything she could have ever written in any of her books. He was deep inside of her but he was still allowing for her to gain excitement from what they were doing together. It just wasn't all one-sided. There were feelings of tenderness with this intimacy.

She slowly tightened her thighs across up hips, pulling his cock even more inside of her and the feeling was unbelievable. She wished it would last forever, but that wasn't going to happen. She already felt the first stirring of her orgasm.

"Forbes, I can't last much longer," she panted holding the headboard tighter.

"Don't fight it. Let it go and I'll be right behind you."

Tossing her head back and closing her eyes, Kissa screamed at the top of her lungs as the world's most perfect orgasm took over her body, blowing every other sexual experience from her life. In the back of her mind she heard Forbes joining her, but she was too exhausted to look at him as she let go of the headboard.

She lay perfectly still as Forbes slid his body from her and she heard dispose of the condom in the trash can next to her bed. A second or two later a wet kiss caressed her temple as his hot body cuddled next to hers in the bed.

"That was indescribable," Forbes breathed against Kissa's ear. "I've never felt this good after making love in my life. I can't wait until we do it again and again and again."

"I think we both need to get some sleep first then try again later on. I'm really worn out. I never knew you had that kind of sexual power."

"Didn't I warn you the day of the shoot I could give you several orgasms in one day?" he reminded her, cupping one firm breast in his hand stroking the nipple with his thumb.

"Yes you did, but I thought you were lying. Men do that you know."

Kissa yelped when Forbes flipped her over and covered her with his sweat covered body. "I'll never lie to you when it comes to my feelings about you," he insisted staring down into her face. "I'll make you feel like the princess that you are and I'll never do anything intentionally to hurt you. We haven't known each other that long, but I'm falling in love with you and I want us to build a future together."

"I'm beginning to have feelings for you too," she confessed running her fingers along the stubble on his jaw. "But let's not rush things, okay?"

"I'm not rushing things. I only want you to know how much you mean to me." Forbes wanted Kissa to understand how he felt before he had to tell her the truth about why he was here.

"Darling, I know and I'm heading in the same direction as you. But how about you get off me and we can try to go to sleep? Because if we don't, I can't promise you I'll be ready to make love again."

Rolling off the little minx that had captured his heart, Forbes snaked his arm around her waist and pulled her against his chest. "Go to sleep and I'll be here when you wake up," he breathed in her ear then planted a kiss below her pierced earlobe.

"Forbes, thank you," she whispered in a sleepy voice.

"For what?" It took Kissa so long to answer Forbes that he thought she might not have heard him.

"For showing me that there are still some good guys left in the world," she answered before she drifted off to sleep.

Her soft-spoken words cut him right to the center of his heart. "Yeah, how long will you feel that away after my true identity comes out?"

Chapter Thirteen

Brad slid down in his car and peeked over the steering at Dru having lunch with some guy he'd never seen before. He didn't understand how she could be laughing and talking with this jerk after being in his office twenty minutes ago. She wasn't supposed to forget about him that quickly.

What happened between them should still be fresh in her mind. Sure, he might have jumped the gun by pushing her away, but he wasn't ready to lose control like that in front of her yet. His feelings for her were so new and unexpected; Dru was the first woman he had ever had gone that far with in his office during the day.

Why couldn't she just have stayed and let him finish what he had to tell her? Brad quickly sat up when Dru's mystery date pulled a box out of his pocket and sat it in front of her.

"I know that isn't a damn ring box," he muttered narrowing his azure eyes on the couple not twenty feet in front of him. "The hell she will marry another guy when I'm madly in love with her." Opening the car door, he got out and stormed over the unsuspecting couple.

"I would have never waited that long if I saw a strange guy giving you a ring box," a half-awake voice confessed by her ear making Kissa almost jump up out of her seat.

"Forbes, you scared the shit out of me," she scolded glancing over her shoulder then planted a kiss on his mouth. "I thought you were still asleep." She turned back around in her seat and saved the new chapter she was working on. "Don't you know better than to sneak up a person like that?"

"I wasn't trying to scare you, but I got lonely in bed and came to find my sexy cuddle partner," he said lifting her out of the leather seat, seating himself in it, and positioning her so she straddled his naked body.

"Forbes, where are your clothes?" she shrieked squirming at the feel of his cock poking at her. Kissa couldn't let him sidetrack her with sex again. Africa wanted the first ten chapters of her book by tomorrow night and Forbes wanting to play house wasn't helping her.

"We don't need clothes for what I have in mind," he whispered sliding his hands under her long t-shirt. "How about I get you out of this and we can make a hot steamy love scene for your next book?"

Her eyes closed at the images Forbes' words conjured in her subconscious, but it wouldn't work. She had to get this last chapter done or Africa would camp out at her house until she got it.

"I can't," she sighed removing his hands off her body and placing them on the arm of the chair. "If I don't email my agent these chapters, she will kill me."

"I'm sure you can think of something to tell her." Leaning forward Forbes ran his tongue across her right nipple sending a pool of moisture between her thighs. "See, even your body agrees with me." Forbes grinned and then arched one dark brown eyebrow. "Why don't you just relax and let me do all of the work?"

Laughing Kissa slid off Forbes before he got her to change her mind and she let him have his way with her for the rest of the night. "Baby, I can't let you do that. I promised Africa these chapters and she'll get them. Because if she doesn't, guess who will be coming over for dinner and not leaving until she does?"

A low manly groan came from deep within Forbes' chest as he stood up and positioned his model perfect body in front of her. "How long will this take? I'm horny and I need a little loving from one adorable woman that has the most exquisite breasts I've ever seen."

"Well Mr. Horny, if you leave me alone for the next hour, I swear I'll help you find a way to resolve your little problem." Kissa giggled at the hard look that passed over Forbes' handsome face.

"Little problem?" he questioned glancing down at his stiff cock. "You shouldn't talk about him like that. You might hurt his feelings then you'll have to kiss and make up."

"I don't mind kissing and making up if he doesn't," she tossed back.

Gray eyes flew to her face as two large hands reached for her. "Come on, let's get started now."

"Stop it, Forbes." Jumping back out of his reach Kissa moved on the other side of the oak wood desk in her office. "You need to leave or there won't be anything going on in an hour."

"Fine," he pouted looking way too cute for his own good. "I'm going, but I'll be back in an hour and you better to ready to live up to that promise." Forbes left the room with his soft threat hanging in the air.

"Please let me keep my heart when it comes to that guy. He's way too cute and charming for his own good." Kissa sighed sitting back down.

"Ms. Abbott, may I speak to you for a moment?"

A mysterious voice vibrated over her skin as Africa dropped the manuscript she was reading. Her mouth opened then snapped shut at the handsome man in her office doorway. She usually didn't work this late, but she had some extra work that she needed to catch up on and now was a good as time as any.

"Do I know you?" she inquired leaning back in her swivel chair. Africa allowed her eyes to travel over the tailored suit that seemed molded to her visitor's perfectly portioned body.

Thick jet black hair fell across one eyebrow over a stunning pair of kelly green eyes and a nice olive complexion complimented the dark suit like nobody's business. She was around attractive men a lot, but this man was in a class all by himself and was arrogant enough to know it.

"No...but we have a mutual friend."

"Mutual friend, may I ask who that is?"

"Forbes Huntington."

Africa's radar went on alert. Who was this guy? A jealous boyfriend or a pissed off ex-employer, she wondered and prayed it was the latter. But with the way the world was nowadays a woman could never tell when it came to a good-looking man.

"How do you know Mr. Huntington?"

"I'm glad you aren't going to deny knowing Forbes," he said coming further into the room.

"Why should I? Has he done something wrong that I need to know about?" Africa asked sitting upright. "If he has, I need to know because we're going to use him a cover model for an upcoming book."

"No, Forbes hasn't done a thing wrong." He stood by an empty chair and looked at her. "Do you mind if I have a seat?"

"Of course not, have a seat Mr....?"

"Zane."

One perfect eyebrow arched. "Is that a first or last name?"

"It's just Zane," came the deep reply as he sat down. "I only wanted to come by and see how much longer you might need my client's service."

"Client?"

"Yes, I'm his manager and I'm trying to book a photo shot for him in Paris, but I don't want it to conflict with his job here."

Africa had a sneaky feeling that Zane wasn't telling her the complete truth about Forbes, but she didn't have to time to dig the honesty out of him tonight. "I don't need him for anything else. We finished up the photo session a couple of days ago."

"Thanks good, so it wouldn't be a problem for me to have him out of here by the end of the month?"

"I don't have a problem with that at all, however Kissa Collins might."

"Who's Kissa Collins?" Zane asked.

"Forbes' girlfriend," she mused. "I'm surprised he didn't tell you about her."

Crossing one leg over another, Forbes' agent gave her a killer smile and said, "Why don't you?"

"I want to give you something."

"I think you gave me several things last night and twice this morning," Kissa laughed kissing Forbes on the cheek as she walked past him.

"No, I'm serious." Catching her by the waist he pulled her down into his lap. "I want to give you something. Do you want it?"

"Of course I want it." She exclaimed looking around for her gift, but she didn't see a box or gift bag in sight. "Where is it?"

"I have it right here." Reaching down next to the chair, Forbes picked up a statue shaped like a computer and keyboard, and handed it to her.

Kissa was a little confused that he made a little trinket seem so important. She thought it was very cute, but she didn't understand what the big deal about it was.

"It's very cute. Thank you." She moved to get off Forbes' lap, but he wrapped his arms around her body preventing her from leaving.

"Open it," he breathed by her ear making her want him again.

As she removed the lid, the sparkle of a diamond ring made her breath catch in her throat. "Forbes, what is it?" she gasped trying not to read too much into his gift.

"I want you to know no matter what happens between us that I will always love you. I'm not asking you to marry me because it's too soon. However, the possibility of you being my wife would make me the happiest man in the world." "Keep this ring close to your heart and when you're ready to give me an answer, I'll be there to hear it. "

Hot tears rained down her cheeks as the beauty of the ring touched her heart. "Are you sure about this? We haven't known each other that long. This is a huge jump. We just started having sex yesterday."

Forbes' warm hands gripped her smaller hands between them, placing them over his heart. "Kissa, I care about you so much. I want to say more, but I can see you aren't ready. You can give this ring as test drive as long as you want, but my feelings are here and now. I was going to give it to you when I snuck into your office last night, but I could see you weren't ready."

"I don't know what to say," she cried staring at the ring then back into his eyes.

"How about you just say thank you and put it on. That's all I'm asking for."

He held his breath while Kissa slipped on the ring he found at the jewelry about two blocks from her house. He rather it be his grandmother's ring that she left him, but it was back home and it would make a better wedding band than engagement ring anyway.

"How about we go and celebrate your new little gift?" he suggested standing up with Kissa in his arms. Forbes wanted to spend as much time with Kissa as he could before his perfect world came shattering down around him.

"Let's go, my hunky cover model," she laughed wrapping her arms around his neck.

"You don't have to tell me twice." Forbes grinned as he left the room, tossing Kissa over his shoulder loving how her sweet laughter made him feel.

Chapter Fourteen

Forbes rolled over on the thick mattress and pulled Kissa's warmth next to him. With the back of his hand, he tenderly brushed a strand of hair away from her eye. "Do you know how much I love you?" he whispered against her forehead. "I never thought when I landed this job I would fall in love with you."

"I love you, too," Kissa answered placing her small hand over his heart.

His heart clenched at Kissa's soft-spoken words. God, he didn't want to hurt this beautiful woman next to him, but his job shouldn't interfere with what they had. He was only doing his job and when it was over things might be a little tense between them, but Kissa would understand.

"You got all silent. Is something wrong?" she asked resting her head on his chest. "Don't you know by now that you can talk to me about anything?"

Not about I'm here to arrest your uncle, he thought as he wrapped his arms around her smooth body. Forbes was beyond worried that she would leave him after she found out about his real job. Most women didn't want to get involved with an F.B.I. agent when they knew going in.

For weeks now he had kept Kissa in the dark so he could be closer to her when her Uncle Thomas got into town. After this case was over he was going to take some time off so he'll be able to work things out with Kissa.

"Honey, there isn't anything wrong. I'm just excited that the two of us are together. It has been such a long time since a woman accepted my career," he lied hating the bad taste it left in his mouth.

"What do you mean?"

"Women love looking at the hot guy on the cover of their favorite romance book, but there are only a few ladies out there strong enough to date us," Forbes explained. "It does get tough when female fans come up to us and move your girlfriend or wife out of the way. Two of my friends got divorced because of the pressure."

"Well, you don't have to worry. Nothing is going to make me leave you. You're stuck with me for a while." Kissa kissed the spot above his left nipple and ran her fingertips over the right one.

Flipping Kissa over, Forbes searched her face and saw all the love she felt for him shining back. "Do you really mean that? You'll stay with me no matter what may happen in the future?"

"Well, unless Johnny Messner comes knocking at my door in the near future, it's safe to say I'll keep you," she teased.

"Kissa, I'm serious. Will you always love me through the good and bad times?" Forbes questioned with more than a hint of concern to his voice. "My world would be over if you ever left me."

"Baby, what's wrong with you?" Kissa sat up beside him concern etched across her beautiful face. She ran his hands over the stubble on his jaw and the caress calmed away most of the tension in his body. "You know that I'm here for you. Are you worried about landing another job?"

If that was only his problem, Forbes wished tugging Kissa back down to his chest. "Bri, I've something to tell you and I don't want you to get upset."

Kissa loved when Forbes called her by her nickname. It sounded so sexy coming from his lips. He was her romance hero come to life, but with a few flaws that every man should have.

"Is it something bad? Do I need to be sitting down instead of lying down to hear your confession? I'm not scared about you have to tell me. It's probably something small that you're blowing out of proportion."

Don't tell her! His mind screamed at him. Kissa's uncle hadn't shown up yet and he might not after all, so he might have a chance to tell her the real reason he came here. He wasn't willing to chance telling Kissa his real job just quite yet.

"Forget about it. I can tell you later." He tucked Kissa's head underneath his chin and covered them with a sheet.

"Are you sure?"

"Yes...let's get some sleep and we can talk in the morning."

Long after Kissa fell asleep beside him, Forbes stayed awake worried about when the shoe was going to drop. Anytime a person was in a relationship and was lying to the other person, the truth came out without warning.

Zane thought he couldn't handle the pressure of dating Kissa and keeping the truth from her, but he could because it was his job. Giving his career his all and being in love with Kissa were two different things. He prayed that she'll be able to separate the two when the time came.

"I love you more than my own life," he whispered to Kissa in the dark. "I hope you understand what I had to do when the time comes."

Flipping the pancakes inside the skillet the next morning, Kissa moved away from the stove and checked on the bacon inside of the microwave then added five more minutes to the time. Last night turned out to be one of the best moments of her life.

Forbes finally told her that he loved her and she was excited about their future, but something was bothering him. He kept twisting and turning around in the bed most of the night. Every time she tried to move away from him last night, he would tug her back against his body.

That wasn't like him. Sure he was a little possessive, but not to the point that she wouldn't leave the bed at night. It was almost like he was afraid she was going to leave him. That's why Forbes' strange behavior lately was bothering her. They had a fantastic relationship and there wasn't one thing she would change about him.

"I'm reading more into it than there is," she muttered to herself as she finished fixing breakfast. Once all the food was done, she dished it up, and placed it in the center of the table.

"Forbes, breakfast is ready," Kissa yelled into the living room. She had never dated a guy who watched the news as much as her boyfriend did. Any chance Forbes got to squeeze in the news, he did.

"I'll be right there, baby," he yelled back at her. "Just two more minutes."

"You better only be two more minutes or I'm not fixing breakfast for you anymore," Kissa threatened, but Forbes knew she was only teasing with him. He had cooked breakfast for the past two weeks. He was just as amazing inside the kitchen as he was in the bedroom. Was there another secret talent Forbes was hiding from her?

The ringing of the phone stopped her mind from wandering down a path it shouldn't. She had made love with Forbes. They both needed time to rest before they went another round.

"I'll get it," she said, picking up the phone of the counter.

"Hello."

"Is this my favorite niece?" A male voice asked with a hint of a southern accent.

"Uncle Thomas," Kissa smiled sitting down at the kitchen table. "How are you doing? Is everything okay?"

"Everything is fine. I'm just going to be in town for a few days and I was wondering if I could drop by while I was here," Thomas asked.

"You know that you never need an invitation. You're more than welcome to stay with me if you want. You're family. I haven't forgotten all the times you let me stay at your place."

"Niece, I'm not staying in town that long. I'll probably only be in Dallas for a few hours then I'm headed on a long planned vacation."

"Oh, I hate to hear that," she pouted disappointed her uncle wouldn't be in town long enough to get to know Forbes. Kissa wanted the two favorite men in her life to be good friends as well.

"I knew you would, but I'll be at your house sometime tomorrow. Is there anything new going on with you? It always seems like you have a surprise to tell me. How's the writing?"

Kissa peeked over her shoulder at Forbes laid out on the couch watching the news. She had a hard time dragging her eyes away from his bare chest and jeans covered legs. He was such a wonderful surprise in her life. Uncle Thomas was going to be so happy for that she finally found the one.

"I've a boyfriend," she whispered into the phone then giggled.

"Niece, please tell me he's better than Hoops was," Thomas complained. "I hated that loser on sight."

"Hoops was only a passing fling. I fell in love with that sandy hair of his and nothing else."

"Are you sure it wasn't because he looked like Rick Fox?"

"Uncle Thomas, please! I was young and made a mistake. After you told me about him I stopped dating him, didn't I?"

"Okay, I'll drop it. What's this new guy's name?"

"Forbes," Kissa sighed with love in her voice, "and you're going to love him."

"Forbes? What is it with you and these guys with these wild names? Can't you date a Jeff or Brian?"

"Uncle Thomas, I'm a writer. I like creative names."

"Fine, Baby K. Will this guy be at your house tomorrow, so I can give him the once over? Can't have any creep winning over my favorite niece's heart."

"I'm your only niece," she laughed.

"That doesn't make a difference. Is he going to be there or not?" Thomas asked.

"Yes, he'll be here and you better be nice or I won't invite you to the wedding," Kissa threatened touching the ring on her finger. She still hadn't told Forbes that she was going to marry him.

"Wedding!" he yelled. "How long have you been seeing this man?"

"A little over a month, but he's the one and we both know it."

"Kissa, don't be rushing into anything that you haven't thought about. Please take more time to get to know this man. He may not be your Prince Charming."

"Uncle Thomas, you remind me so much of daddy when you said that," she sighed remembering how her father constantly told her to stop letting her heart rule her emotions instead of common sense.

"Baby K, I'm not liking what I'm hearing. I'll come over later on today. I need to see what this man has to offer you. Don't go anywhere I'll be there in about three hours." Her uncle ended the call before she could stop him.

She wasn't ready for Forbes to meet her only living relative yet, but it didn't seem like she had much of a choice about it now. She got up from the table and strolled into the living room. "Forbes, you need to get up and take a shower. We have company coming."

"Who is it? An ex-boyfriend coming back to tell you he's madly in love with you?" Forbes asked turning his head to stare at her.

"No," she said shaking her head. "It's my Uncle Thomas and he wants to meet you."

Forbes body went on high alert. His heart fell to his feet as Kissa's words sank into his head. It couldn't be time. He wasn't ready to come clean with the truth yet. What was he going to do? This might he his only chance to catch Thomas Collins and Zane would kill him if he didn't take it. Shit, he had to find a way to get Kissa out of the house the second her uncle got here. He could have Zane and the rest of the Bureau on standby to move in moment Kissa was out of the line of fire. Losing her wasn't a part of the plan and he had to make sure it wouldn't happen.

"Your uncle is coming?" he asked getting up off the couch. "I didn't know that's who you were talking to on the phone. I thought he wasn't a big part of your life."

Kissa joined him on the couch and he wrapped her up against his chest. "I love my uncle a lot. He's my daddy's twin and the only family member I have left. He's a gypsy," she chuckled.

"A gypsy?" Forbes frowned while trying to think of a way to get Kissa to leave the house.

"Yep, he moves from place to place without a care in the world. I wish I could do that. I'm very jealous that he can."

"You do that with your writing."

"I guess I do a little, but Uncle Thomas can never seem to hold down a job, but he's never without money. I never understood how he did that. Once I asked him about it and he told me that he was a banker robber."

Leaning away from Kissa, Forbes' shocked eyes fell down to her face. "You're uncle is a bank robber?" Shit, he couldn't let Zane find out that Kissa knew about this. He'll want to send her off to prison along with her uncle.

"God, don't tell me you believe that silly story! One time he told me he was a pirate and then a male stripper," Kissa said rolling her eyes. "He's very good at storytelling and I think I get my writing gene from him. He worked for a newspaper for a while, but he hated the hours and quit."

I bet he did, Forbes thought.

"Honey, you know that we have a problem."

"What kind of problem do we have, Mr. Huntington? Don't you want to meet my crazy and over the top Uncle Thomas?"

"Kissa, I love you and want to me any person you want to introduce me to, but we don't have any food in the house. Remember we were going to the store when the phone rang?" Crossing his fingers behind his back, Forbes prayed that Kissa fell for the bait.

"Shit, you're right," she retorted standing up. "We have to get some food in the house, but I don't want to miss my uncle."

"Kissa, don't get in a panic. How about I stay here and wait for your uncle. We can get to know each other while you're gone?"

Big bright brown eyes sparkled with love the second before Kissa stood on tiptoes and wrapped her arms around his neck. "Baby, I love you so much! That's a perfect idea. I can get the stuff for my famous Italian chicken with sausage and peppers and I can fix peach cobbler for dessert."

Forbes knew that meal would never get fix and this might be the last time Kissa told him that she loved him, but he had to do his job. "Sweetheart, why don't you go ahead and leave so you can beat the afternoon traffic. I promise I'll be nice to your uncle when he gets here." He couldn't say the same for Zane and the rest of the men in the Bureau.

"Alright," she agreed grabbing her purse off the chair by the couch. "I'll try not to be longer than an hour." Kissa gave him a soft kiss then went out the door, closing it softly behind her.

Going to the window Forbes waited until Kissa was around the corner then went over to use her phone. The man he called picked up on the first ring. He didn't wait a second before the words were out of his mouth.

"Our suspect is on his way. I advise you to get everyone over here ASAP." Forbes hung up the phone and shoved his relationship with Kissa to the back of his mind; it was now time to deal with business and not his emotions.

Chapter Fifteen

"Oh, my God," Kissa muttered as she turned the corner that led to her street. There was at least a dozen or more cars lined up in front of her house and even a few parked on the grass. Finding an empty parking spot a couple of houses down from her, she shut off her car and got out racing towards her house.

What had happened while she was gone to the store? Panic lodged in her throat as she got closer to her house. Did something happen to Forbes or her uncle while she was gone? She wouldn't be able to take it if one of them were hurt. Kissa tried to rush past a man wearing a dark blue suit blocking her open front door, but he grabbed her by the arm.

"Ma'am, where do you think you're going?" he demanded loudly in her face.

"Let go of me," she hissed jerking her arm away. "This is my house and I've a right to know what's going on here. Has something happened to my Uncle Thomas or Forbes?"

"You're Kissa Collins," the man wearing the suit asked looking her up and down. "You look different than your picture," he muttered so low that she almost didn't hear him.

"What are you talking about?" she demanded shoving past him going inside. "Uncle Thomas, Forbes, where are you?" Kissa yelled hurrying through the house with the man at her heels.

Not seeing them downstairs, she cut through the living room and raced upstairs.

"Miss Collins, stop right there," the man yelled after her. "You can't go up there."

Kissa kept moving in the direction that she heard the voices coming from. She could hear her uncle and Forbes yelling at each other the closer that she got. She didn't know what all these people were doing her, but hell or high water, she was going to find out.

※

"Does my niece even know who you really are?" Thomas Collins yelled at him. "I know that she loves me too much to set me up like that. She believed you were a model. What is she going to do when she finds out the truth? I know Kissa; she won't have anything to do with you."

"Mr. Collins, you need to keep your mouth shut," Forbes snapped. "You're a criminal and have no business talking about my life. You're going away for a very long time."

"Was part of your cover making my niece fall in love with you?" Thomas accused as if he hadn't spoken a word. "She's going to hate you for this. You're finished with her. My niece will never say another word to you when she finds out."

"You know nothing. Kissa and I will be fine. She'll understand that I was just doing my job. She's loves me and I love her. We'll get through this, but I don't have to discuss this with you."

"Oh, but you do Mr. F.B.I. agent because you're here in my face and you can't leave until another one of your friends come up here to get me. How did you get Kissa to leave so you could arrest me?"

Forbes hated that he was allowing Thomas to get under his skin but it couldn't be helped. Kissa's uncle knew all the right buttons to push and it was pissing him off. However, he wasn't going to allow Thomas Collins bad mouth opinions to ruin what he knew Kissa felt for him.

"I sent her to the store after something. I loved her enough that I didn't want her to be here when this happened. By the time she gets back all of my men will be cleared out and I can tell her what happened. Plus, you won't be around to fill her head with lies about me. I know that she loves you, but she loves me more and will understand."

A smug look came over Thomas's face. "You think so? My niece will overlook the fact that you made her fall in love with you to get closer to me?"

"I know that she will," Forbes replied confidant. "Kissa is in love with me."

❦

"Mr. Huntington, you don't know as much as you think you do," a soft yet furious voice hurled behind him.

Forbes spun around and then stumbled back as Kissa's slapped almost knocked him to the floor. "You lying son of bitch." She lunged at him again, but Zane grabbed her yanking her arms behind her back.

"Miss. Collins, you're under arrest for hitting a Federal agent."

"I don't care. Let me go so I can hit him again. He's a mendacious bastard and that light tap didn't hurt him," she hissed twisting at her arms as she tried to get free.

Shaking off the ringing in his ears Forbes watched Kissa struggle against Zane's strong hold. "Let her go. I'm not going to press charges." He glared at his boss at the way he was handling Kissa. She was hurt and upset, but she wasn't a danger to him.

"I can't do that."

He shoved down the burst of anger the consumed him and tried again. "Zane, I said let Kissa go. She isn't going to hit me again," Forbes muttered, rubbing his stinging cheek. "I deserved the slap anyway."

"I'll hit you again as soon as this jerk let's go of my arms," Kissa threatened.

"No, you won't." Forbes stated moving to stand in front of her. He saw the brave image she was trying to put on; however, he saw the hurt in her once adoring eyes.

Big brown eyes glistened with unshed tears as Kissa stared back at him before jerking her head away. "I hate you," she whispered under her breath, but he still heard her and her words cut deep.

"You no good bastard," Thomas yelled at him from across the room making him focus his attention back on him instead of Kissa. "Leave my niece alone. She isn't a plaything for you to use."

"Zane, can you take care of Mr. Collins while I speak to his niece alone."

His boss looked back and forth between Kissa and Thomas for a span of two minutes before he let her go of her arms and took her uncle from the room.

"Kissa, let me explain." The words were out of his mouth as soon as they were alone. The longer he waited to explain his actions the harder it would be to get Kissa to listen.

"Agent Huntington, I don't want you to explain anything to me." She turned away from him.

Forbes wrapped his hand around Kissa's. "Don't leave. We need to talk." He hated the pleading sound of his voice, but he had to make Kissa listen to him.

"Please let go of my arm," she hissed giving it a hard jerk.

"No." Forbes eased past Kissa's body blocking her only way out. He couldn't permit her leave until they talked and found a way to resolve this problem.

"Are you holding me here to question me about my uncle?"

"Your uncle isn't the reason I wanted you to stay and you know it," Forbes replied releasing Kissa's arm. "I want to know how much damage I've caused to our relationship."

"Relationship," Kissa snickered facing him. "I was a means to an end for you. You only faked a relationship with me to get closer to my uncle. How do I even know if Forbes Huntington is your real name?"

"It is."

"Do you think I'm actually going to believe a word that comes out of your deceitful mouth?" Kiss stared at him like he had grown a second head.

"I'm not lying to you, baby. I'm in love with you."

The only sound in the room was the clock clicking on the far left wall while Forbes waited for Kissa to answer him. She had to understand that he was only doing his job and their love was independent from his work.

He'd have asked her out at a night club or any other place he saw her because she was an attractive woman. It was just turned out to be bad luck his job was the reason he came to Dallas. After all the dust settled, she'll realize what they shared was special and only came around once in a life time.

Kissa gave him a watery smile as tears filled her eyes. "No. You don't love me because if you had you would have told me the truth weeks ago."

"I was doing my job. Your Uncle Thomas is a bank robber and he had to be apprehended."

He was sick of defending his actions. Thomas Collins couldn't stay on the street and he was glad he did his job. The only thing that pained him was Kissa got hurt in the process. "I did what was right."

"You're right. You did what was right for you and now I'm going to do the same thing," Kissa agreed. "I'm ending things between us. None of it was real anyway, so the both of us should be able to go back to our old lives without any problems." Brushing past him Kissa hurried out the door before he got a chance to stop her.

"I'm not giving up on us!" Forbes yelled after her. "You mean too much to me."

"Fuck you!" she screamed back then disappeared around the corner.

He hurried around the corner and down the steps shoving Zane out of his way in time to see Kissa climb into her car and speed off. Forbes started after her until an iron grip closed over his upper arm.

"You don't have time to go after her. You're needed back at the office to fill out the report then I need you in the room when I talk with Mr. Collins."

"Zane, you can do all of that without me. I'm not going to lose her." Forbes tried to loosen his boss's grip but it wasn't working.

"Don't make me fire you on the spot. You never did one thing by the book when it came to this case, but damn it to hell, you're going to follow orders this time!"

He couldn't argue with Zane. "Shit, I hate this," he growled tossing his head back. "I'll finish up what you want me to then I'm taking a leave of absence until I get her back in my life. I refuse to let this ruin what we have."

"You're really in love with her?" Zane realized as he let go of his arm and stepped back.

"Kissa is the woman I've been searching for, and I know deep down, if I have the chance, I can get her back. I just need the time to make her understand she can't throw away what we shared."

Chapter Sixteen

"Oh, my God, this is so beautiful," Dru gushed picking up the ring box staring at square cut diamond. "Are you sure about this? Have you given it a lot of thought?"

"I know that I'm in love and can't imagine not spending another moment without..."

"You're going to have to spend it without Dru, because you aren't going to marry her," a loud voice growled next to them.

The ring was ripped out of her hand and flung back on the table. "Dru, I won't let you marry this guy. What's wrong with you? We have one fight and you're willing to jump into another's guys arms," Brad accused squatting down next to her chair. "You meant the world to me and I'll fight to the end for you."

Dru fell back against her seat taken back by Brad had followed her. What had gotten into him lately? She wasn't used to all of this attention from him. "Did you follow me?"

"Yeah and I'm glad I did. Who is this loser and why is he giving you a ring?"

"Buddy, I don't know who you are but you need to stop calling me a loser," her lunch companion snapped at Brad.

"I'll call you anything I want," Brad threatened standing up to his full six foot six inch height. "Dru is mine and I'm not about to give her up without a fight."

"Brad, stop!" she hissed pulling at his arm. "You don't know what you're doing. Listen to me."

Brad jerked his arm away from her. "No. I need to show this guy who you belong with and it isn't him."

"Of course I don't belong with him," Dru grounded out jumping up from her chair. "Luke is my first cousin, you idiot," she shouted drawing attention over to their table.

"First cousin," Brad muttered turning to face her, "if he's your cousin why was he giving you a ring?"

"I wanted Dru's opinion about the size and if Bianca would like it," Luke cut in moving to stand by her. "God man, you've a temper problem. I don't know why my cousin thinks she in love with you."

"Can't you stop working on that book for one minute and talk to me?" Africa asked closing her laptop and moving it away from her.

Kissa held her tongue until she gained control of her temper. "You'd better be glad I have that set to save every two minutes or you would be on my Most Wanted list right now."

Africa laughed at her before dropping on the couch next to her. "You aren't going to hide away in here forever. Even a ground hog comes out to see his shadow."

"I don't have any reason to go outside for anything. My book has a deadline. You're my agent. Shouldn't you be pushing me to get this done down and off to the publisher?"

"Kissa, you know they have to go with another cover because of Forbes, so they gave you an extra thirty days to finish."

The sympathy in her friend's voice made her bolt from the couch. "How many times do I've to tell you I don't want to hear his name?"

"I think what he did was horrible and uncalled for, but don't let it ruin your life."

"How can you say that?" Kissa shouted. "Forbes used me as bait to lure my uncle to my house. He slept with me so I would fall for him, making it easier to place the binders over my eyes." Kissa wrapped her arms around her body at the sudden chill in the room.

"Bri, I think you're judging Forbes too hard. Zane told me that he wanted to come clean with you on numerous times."

"Zane, told you," she hissed through clenched teeth. "What in the hell are you doing talking to that bastard?"

"He has been calling to check on you for Forbes. I was angry at first and wanted to protect you until I realized how much Forbes really does care about you."

She couldn't believe this shit. Africa was supposed to be her best friend; however she wasn't acting like it. "How can you turn on me like this? Isn't your girlfriend supposed to have your back during a bad break-up?"

Africa got up and tried to touch her, but she stepped back.

"Don't touch me. You aren't the friend I thought you were." Kissa ignored the hurt look that crossed Africa's exotic features.

"I'm going to forget you said that because you're in pain."

"You have it so wrong. I'm not in pain. Forbes has pissed me off and I feel stupid for falling for him. I wasn't in love with the guy. He was good to look at and even better in bed, but it wasn't going to grow into anything deeper." Hopefully, Africa would believe her lie giving her the ability to think it was true.

"Have you gotten lost in the writing world so much that you can't feel you own emotions?" Africa challenged dragging her back down to the couch. "You're still in love with Forbes and it's not going to get any easier until you talk to him."

"NO!" Kissa screamed. The need to race from the room ate at her, but she stayed seated. "Hell will freeze over before I say anything to that gray-eyed bastard."

"Bri, listen to me."

"Can you please leave me alone? I'm getting a headache and I want to take a nap because I still have three more chapters to finish tonight." Africa opened her mouth, but she interrupted her, "Will you just go?"

"Fine, I'll let you get some rest." Standing up her agent and best friend looked her like she had never seen her before. "This isn't healthy for you. All this anger isn't you. Bri, you need to work through it and find the sweet girl I know that you are." Africa walked away from her and went out the door closing it with a soft click.

"I was a sweet girl until I had the misfortune to meet Agent Forbes Huntington and my life went downhill after that," she sighed in the empty room.

"You look like hell. Is Kissa still not talking taking your calls?"

Forbes slid over on the bench so Zane could sit down next to him. He hadn't been at work for almost two weeks and he was actually thinking about not returning. "I took a trip back to Dallas last week. She wouldn't even open the door for me. The last time I saw her was at her uncle's trial."

"I even tried to speak to her then but she was with her agent and Africa was like a mama bear protecting her cub. She rushed Kissa out of the court past the cameras into a waiting car and then left."

"She still can't be mad at you, and if she is then you don't need her."

"Zane, shut the hell up! You don't know what I need. Kissa understood me and I loved it. We could look across at room at each other and know what the other one was thinking. Now I've lost all of that and I doubt that I'll ever get it back."

"Are you sure that you can't try talking to her again?" Zane suggested. "Kissa can't hate you forever. You just played the role your job called for. She should get that since she's a writer. Most of her time is writing about people she isn't and she makes a comfortable living at it too."

Forbes laughed at his boss' reasoning for him lying to Kissa and it eased some of the pain from his heart. "I love the way you think about things, but Kissa doesn't see it like that. Thomas was the only family she had left and the man she was in love with helped put him away."

"Her uncle decided to take on a life of crime and that's what got him locked away not you," his boss corrected. "Kissa is a grown woman not a child. She needs to understand stuff happens in life and move on. If she truly loves you then she needs to get over it and find you."

A part of him knew Zane was speaking the truth, yet he wasn't ready to give up on winning Kissa back and taking all the blame for their current tribulations. "I'm going to try one more time and see what happens. She's having a book signing next week and I'm going to be there."

"Do you think she'll talk to you?"

"I won't know until I get there."

"I'll come with you," Zane offered.

Forbes frowned. "Why? You aren't Kissa's biggest fan."

"Someone needs to keep Africa away from the two of you. You can't have any privacy with her lurking in the shadows."

Swallowing down a grin Forbes rose from the bench. "Africa is a very tough woman; she isn't going to let you charm her."

Zane snickered. "I don't want Africa. She isn't even my type. I offered to go as backup for you and that's it." His boss rose and patted him on the shoulder. "I'm not interested in Kissa's agent so get that out of your mind."

"That's good to hear, because she can't stand you either," he tossed back then walked away.

"Why doesn't she like me?" Zane yelled after him but he kept going like he never heard a word.

Chapter Seventeen

One week later

"Kissa, stop it," Africa scolded as she got up and paced around the small room for the tenth time in the span of only a few minutes. "There's a least a hundred people out there to see you and you're already a bundle of nerves. You aren't going to have a steady hand to sign your name if you keep this up."

"Why are you on my case?" she complained flopping down in the fold out chair by the window. The sunlight shined through warming up her and soothing the anxiety that was clawing its way through her body. This was her first book signing and she hoped everything would go perfectly.

Forbes hadn't contacted her in week and that pleased her despite what Africa thought. She wasn't in love with him anymore. All of his things that were left at her house were packed up and donated to the local Goodwill Store. Since he was a federal agent, he probably had a closet full of disposable clothes. A man like him had to be ready to run at a moment's notice. Why would he bring anything of value with him?

She just never thought she would lose her heart so easily the first day Forbes appeared in her life. Why hadn't her womanly instinct kicked in and warned her away from him?

Kissa silently scolded herself then shook it off. No, she wasn't going to blame herself for this.

Agent Huntington was trained to make people bend to his wants and needs. Without a doubt, he had spent years crafting his charisma making it a lot easier for him to seduce unsuspecting females. Honestly, how many men in the Bureau looked like Forbes? He oozed the bad boy sex appeal. The instant her eyes landed on Forbes, she fell hard for him like Jennifer Gray did for Patrick Swayze in Dirty Dancing.

"I'm such an idiot," she chastised herself. "Why couldn't I let it stay strictly business between us?"

"Bri, you aren't an idiot. You're a woman who fell for a man," Africa corrected as she came across the room and kneeled down in front of her. "I know you want to go cold turkey when it comes to you-know-who, but it isn't working for you."

Kissa smiled at Africa but she wasn't buying her friend's excuse. "Thanks, but I'm not talking to Forbes. He doesn't understand what he did was wrong. He never thought about being honest with me."

"How do you know that? Have you given him a chance to explain?"

"Africa, two weeks ago I was in court watching my favorite uncle on trial for being one of the F.B.I.'s ten most wanted bank robbers," Kissa muttered, hurt pouring from her voice. "Besides, when Forbes tried to approach me you practically dragged me down the court house steps."

Standing up Africa moved away. "I know and I feel bad about that now, but you were so upset that day. I couldn't let Forbes corner you."

A knock on the door interrupted them. "Come in," Kissa yelled standing up.

The bookstore owner came in with a huge smile that covered her sienna face. Her thick braids were pulled back from her head with a clip. Kissa had liked Kay the second they were introduced.

"We are ready for you, Miss Collins," she stated. "I can't believe that I've already sold every copy of your book I had in the store."

"Are you sure?" she questioned.

"Yes, I sold out your newest hardcover book in a matter of minutes," Kay answered, "then they started on the mass market books."

Kissa was speechless. She never thought people would respond to her like this at her first book signing. "How many people are out there now?" She wasn't fond of big crowds, but she could deal with one if the time called for it.

"It's hard to guess, but I would say over a hundred."

Lord, give me the strength, she prayed silently.

"You can do this," Africa said giving her encouragement. "Just take a deep breath and smile. Don't make it worse than it is. Remember that I'm going to be standing right behind you."

I can do this. I can do this. I can do this. She kept saying that over and over in her head until her pulse returned to a normal rate. Kissa knew she wasn't a coward and her fans were waiting. It was be very disappointing if she didn't get out there.

"Okay, I'm ready. Lead me to them."

"Wonderful," Kay grinned turning back towards the door. "Thank you again for coming here and doing this."

"Shades of Love was the first book store to place my books on its shelves. How could I say no? You helped me gain the fans that I've today."

"I may have given them the avenue to buy your books, but your excellent writing keeps them coming back." Kay opened the door allowing her and Africa to walk through then she followed.

"Thank you for the compliment," Kissa exclaimed.

Kay waved off her statement. "Don't thank me for speaking the truth. Now, let's go and give your fans what they want."

"What do they want?" she asked growing a little more nervous as they strolled towards the front of the store.

"The chance to meet the famous Kissa Collins," Africa answered. She wrapped her arm around her shoulder and gave it a light squeeze. "Push everything else to the back of your mind and enjoy this."

Turning her head slightly, Kissa glanced up at her friend. "I'll try my best."

"There she is," Forbes whispered as he watched Kissa take a seat at the empty table that only twenty minutes ago was filled with her latest book. Her fans had snatched the books up like they were worth a million dollars. Luckily, he got here a little early and was about to get one before they were all gone.

He couldn't take his eyes off how the white sundress contrasted with Kissa's dark beauty. Everything about her looked so bewitching today; if he wasn't already in love with her, he would have fallen hard today.

What was he going to do if she never looked at him the same way again? He wasn't ready to think about all the time he had been cheated away from her. These past few weeks had been the worst of his life. Every day he remembered how her warm body felt against his chest, how sometimes her fingers stroked the middle of his chest until she fell asleep. From looking at her sitting so calm, no one would ever guess how she loved taking over the bed in her sleep.

Her body continually sought his out during the night until she found the position she was most comfortable in. Forbes growled deep in his throat when Kissa smiled up at an attractive man while she signed his book.

"If you don't stop that someone is going to look at you strangely," Zane laughed beside him.

"Shut up!"

"Don't yell at me. I'd be over there with her if she were mine."

"She isn't yours," he hissed, hating that the fact the Kissa wasn't his either.

"The last time I checked Kissa wasn't yours either, Agent Huntington." Zane snickered. "I'm not going to stand here and watch you drool over Miss Collins. I'm going next door to get something to eat," his boss tossed out his parting comment then was out the door.

"I'm going to try everything in my power to make her mine again," Forbes stated as he stood at the back of the line. He had to make sure that Kissa didn't bolted the second she laid eyes on him.

"Do you need me to go and get you something? You don't look that good," Africa whispered by her ear. "You haven't moved for a while and I know you have to be thirsty."

"Oh, I would love a Cherry Coke from next door," Kissa answered replied giving her fan back the autographed book.

"I'll try to get back as soon as I can. Do you want something to eat, too?"

"That's okay. I'll eat after I'm done here. I only have about eight people left."

"Alright, I'm outta of here." Her agent patted her on her shoulder before moving towards the front of the bookstore.

Kissa watched Africa leave the building with a little bit of envy. She loved being her with all of her fans, but her wrist was starting to hurt and she was just plain tired. Africa didn't know she wasn't sleeping at night. As much as she tried to hate Forbes for everything that he did to her, she still had some feelings for him.

He seemed to know what she was thinking without a word being spoken. One time after she had spent over eight hours in front of the computer working on her book, after she logged off, Forbes had fixed her a bath and afterwards he massaged her down with scent oil until she fell asleep.

Some nights they wouldn't even make love, but just cuddle and listen to music. Kissa's eyes started to tear up when it dawned on her that all of it was an act of his part. Forbes never cared about it. From the second he introduced himself, it all had been about tossing her uncle into jail and sending him away for the rest of his life.

"Miss Collins, are you okay?" a female fan asked as she handed the book back to her.

Kissa blinked a couple of times to dry her eyes and gave the lady a small smile. "Yes, I'm fine. Thank you for asking."

"Okay, you just looked like you were a million miles away," her fan replied. "By the way, I totally loved you latest book. Are you planning to do one about Brad and Dru?"

"Yes, I'm working on them."

"Wonderful, I'll be the first one in line to buy it." The woman waved at her then walked away allowing the next fan to move up.

The flow of fans stayed steady for about the next twenty minutes and Kissa chatted with them and answered all of their questions. All of them were excited to know that Brad and Dru would be getting their own story and she was pleased to know they wanted Brad and Dru's story told. She only hoped she could do it justice now since in her mind Brad looked like Forbes, and it was hard to write about in a romantic way.

However, she was a writer and it was her job to be able to separate fact from fiction. Forbes wasn't going to ruin this story for her. She had wanted to write about this couple for the past two years and they would get the happy ending that they deserved.

A hand touching her shoulder drew her attention away from her signing the book in front of her. Glancing over her shoulder, she saw Kay standing there. "Do you want to take a break and come back in a few minutes?"

"Can you see how many people are still in line?"

Kay moved to the end of the table and looked at the line. "I only see about four more people and you should be finished for the day."

"No, that's okay. I'll just stay here and sign the rest of them."

"Can I get you anything?

"No, Africa should be coming back with my drink in a few minutes. She went next door to get it."

"She's probably still standing in line with the lunch hour crowd. That restaurant is the hottest spot in town and is standing room only," Kay said, giving her a concerned look. "Are you positive I can't get you something? I've some bottle water or soft drinks in my office."

"No, thank you."

"Well...if you say so." Kay paused and looked at her for a split second then moved away.

Kissa thought Kay's kindness was sweet, but she didn't want anything. She wished that she hadn't agreed to this book signing. Her publisher had been pushing her to do one for a while but she kept saying no. The only reason she agreed to this was Forbes. She thought meeting her fans would get him out of her mind, but it didn't work. It was like she felt his presence around her and it was driving her crazy.

She was taking a leave of absence after she typed The End on Brad and Dru's story. A long vacation on a tropical beach was so in her future. Africa wasn't going to give her a problem about it either. Oh, just thinking about lying on a beach with a fruity drink in her hand brought a smile to her face.

Shaking off the trance, Kissa focused her attention back on the remaining fans that were still standing there to meet her.

"Good afternoon, thank you for coming to my book signing," Kissa said, taking a book from a woman who looked in her early forties.

"I'm so happy that you finally decided to do one. I have all of your books and I can't wait until your next one comes out," the lady gushed. "Your alpha males are so hot! I dream about leaving my husband all the time for one of the men in your book."

She tried to laugh at the woman's enthusiasm, If she only knew the men in my books don't exist in the world. "I'll tell you a little secret," Kissa whispered to the woman, secretly happy this was her last book to sign for the day. If this lady hadn't been the last person in line she would have lost her mind.

"Oh, what is it?" Her fan took the book back and held it against her ample chest. "I love hearing secrets."

"I wish sometimes that the men in my books were real too. What woman doesn't want to get swept away by her Prince Charming?"

Nodding the lady replied, "I know what you mean. I love my husband, but sometimes I wished he was a little more romantic."

"As long as your husband doesn't lie to you, he's a keeper."

"No, Victor isn't a liar. My husband is one of the most honest guys I've ever meet."

"Then like I said he's a keeper," Kissa sighed wishing Forbes would disappear from her mind and was overwrought that he didn't.

A smile lit up the woman's face bringing a glow to it and taking off five years. "I'm not ever letting him go, but dreams are nice too."

"Yes, they are," she agreed.

"I better go. Victor is taking me out to dinner tonight." The woman waved at her and left.

Closing her eyes Kissa rested her head back against the chair and thanked God for allowing everything to go so smoothly. She had been worried something crazy might happen. She truly wasn't fond of large crowds and today's crowd turned out to be enormous. She never thought that many people would show up to see her.

"Excuse, can I still get an autograph," a masculine voice asked sending a proverbial jolt through her body.

It couldn't be!

Kissa's eyes shot open and she almost fell out of her seat when her gaze connected with Forbes. Damn...Double damn!

Why did his ass have to be so fine? A white t-shirt stretched across his chest and the jeans she loved him in hugged his lower body. Even his five o'clock shadow was turning her on more than it usually did.

The familiar musky scent of his cologne filled her nose, it made her body throb for what they once had, but would never have again. She shoved the thoughts of the past to the back of her mind and refocused.

"What in the hell are you doing here? I didn't see you in the store or in line."

"I stepped behind one of the bookshelves when there were two people ahead of me," Forbes answered. "I knew if you saw me before now it would be over."

"You're damn right," she hissed. "I want you to leave. The sight of you makes me sick."

"No...I came to get an autograph and that's what I want," he said tossing her book on the table.

Opening the book Kissa scribbled something inside and flung it back at the man who had literally ripped her heart out of her chest. "There you go. Now get the hell away from me."

Forbes grabbed the book and read the inscription. "I didn't think you knew that kind of language," he laughed tossing the book back on the table. "I know you hate me but if you let me..."

"Please don't tell me you want to explain anything to me, Agent Huntington, I wouldn't believe a word that came out of your mouth. You're a liar and will always be one."

"Forbes."

Kissa's eyes narrowed on the man in front of her. "What?"

"My name is Forbes...not Agent Huntington when I'm around you."

"You were Forbes when I thought you were my boyfriend," Kissa corrected. "Since you aren't anything to me now, calling you Agent Huntington just seemed right."

"I can be something to you again if you let me."

Kissa snickered and it even sounded evil to her own ears. "I wouldn't let you give me a glass of water if I was dying from thirst. What you did to me was cold and heartless. I'll have that memory for the rest of my life."

Forbes rushed around the table blocking her against the wall. "Baby, listen to me. I want to find what we used to have. I'm begging you for a second chance."

"Fuck no!" she screamed in his face. "I hate you and never want to see you again."

Forbes flinched then ran his fingers through his hair. She remembered him doing the same thing after they made love. It was so silky that it seemed unfair for a man to have it, however she played with it until she fell asleep.

"Kissa, I'm leaving in two days for another job and I don't know when I'm going to be back."

Lord, was he going to do something dangerous and get himself hurt? She couldn't let Forbes know that she still cared about him.

"So, I could care less."

"Stop lying to me," Forbes snapped grabbing her by the arms.

"Let go of me."

"Not until you tell me that I still have a chance with you," he demanded jerking her fully against his chest.

"Has hell frozen over? That's the only way I'll tell you something like that."

"Bri, I know you still love me, I can see it in your eyes," Forbes challenged.

"Look closer…that is called hatred. I hate you Agent Forbes Huntington. You ruined my life."

Chapter Eighteen

Panic laced through his heart as Kissa's words settled into his soul. He wasn't going to get a second chance with her. The woman he had been wanting for all of his life despised the sight of him.

"You don't mean this," he said trying to reason with her. Kissa was just hurt and it was causing her to lash out at him. "I know you're still in love with me, because I'm still in love with you."

"How dare you come here and say that to me? You don't know the meaning of the word love!"

"I know that every time I see you, my heart lodges in my throat. You are the last thing I think about before I go to sleep at night and the first thing on my mind when I wake up," Forbes said trying to make Kissa understand how he still felt about her.

"God, you're so good. How long did it take for you to come up with that?" she snickered. "It sounds like something I would write in one of my romance novels. Have you been sneaking at peek at some of them?"

He didn't like this nasty side of Kissa. It wasn't her. She was sweet and understanding. She wasn't the type to have a nasty retort at the tip of her tongue, especially for him, not after all the things they shared together.

"No...I meant every word from my heart. Kissa, you know that I love you. Why do you think I gave you the ring? I want to marry you. I know you still want the same thing too." Forbes let go of Kissa and took a step back from her.

"Thank, God," she sighed. "I thought you would never get your hands off me." Kissa brushed at her arms like his touched disgusted her. "When are you going to get it through your head that I don't want you anymore?"

He would never get it through his head because it was a lie. "Bri, I know you're upset with me right now, so I'm going to leave. However, I'm not giving up on us. What we found with each other is rare and I'm not letting you brush it under the rug."

"Go away, Forbes," Kissa muttered turning her back to him.

"I don't know how many times I've to say I'm sorry about your uncle, but I am," Forbes apologized. "I'll say it another hundred if it will get you to look at me the way you used to. Kissa, I love you and I always will."

Standing behind Kissa, the urge to wrap her in his arms clawed at Forbes, but he fought it. It wouldn't do any good for him to rush her back into his life. After all the mistrust and hurt evaporated, Kissa would be her old self and hopefully back in his life.

"I'm leaving," he said moving around the table, "but I'll be back before I've to leave on my next assignment. I love you with all my heart Kissa, please never forget that." Forbes turned on his heel and went out the door without looking back.

Kissa watched Forbes retreating back with mixed feelings. On one hand, she felt like he truly he loved her and wanted to spend the rest of his life with her. But on the other hand, could she really forget the ultimate betrayal?

"Kissa, are you okay?" Kay asked appearing at her side. "I saw you talking to that man and you looked so upset. I didn't know if I should interrupt or not."

"It's okay, Kay," Kissa muttered as she watched Forbes through the bookstore window. "I know him." She was having such a hard time trying to sort through her feelings for Forbes.

"He's very handsome. Is he someone special to you?"

"No...he was just a man that I used to know."

"Well...from the way he was looking at you, I think he doesn't want to be," Kay exclaimed.

"I'm not sure that can ever happen," Kissa answered looking over at Kay. "Some things just aren't meant to be."

"Never say never. The first time I met my husband I thought he was a world class jerk until I got to know him. Now we're about to celebrate our fifteenth year wedding anniversary and my love grows for him more each day."

Kissa couldn't believe that Kay thought she wanted to marry Forbes. "Why do you think I want to a relationship with Forbes? I never said that."

"I'm hope I'm not speaking out of terms, but for a woman who's not interested in a man, your eyes never left him until he disappeared from sight. If I'm wrong I apologize, but if I'm right you should give him a chance."

"Even if he lied to me?" she whispered.

"Hey, I don't need to know that whole story because it's not any of my business. All I'm saying it that man who just left looked like a man ready to spend the rest of his life with you," Kay informed her before walking away.

"I just don't know," Kissa muttered gathering up her stuff off the table. "A part of me wants to forgive Forbes, but the other part of me wants to cut and run." As she left the signing area and went back toward the back of the building, Kissa wondered what happened to Africa and her drink she was supposed to bring her.

"How many times do I've to tell you to leave me alone?" Africa tried brushing past the man in front of her, but he wasn't moving. "I think what you and Forbes did to Kissa was horrible."

"We were only doing our jobs," Zane stated.

"So, your job was to break my best friend's heart, rush into her house and arrest her uncle while she was gone to the store? Couldn't it all been handled in a better way?"

"Forbes told us to wait until we saw Kissa leave before we rushed the house. He had hoped all of it would be over before she got by home, but it didn't work out like that."

"Are you saying that makes it okay?"

"I'm saying we were sent here to arrest a bank robber, and that is what we did. Kissa shouldn't hate Forbes for that. He couldn't help that he fell in love with her."

Africa couldn't believe the nerve of Zane. He was trying to act like Kissa should forgive Forbes for deceiving her for weeks. Why didn't men understand that women hated when a relationship started off with a lie?

"You're unbelievable," she complained stepping back. "Bri isn't the wrong party here. Forbes is and he needs to leave her alone. My friend isn't about to get over this anything soon."

Zane chuckled at her. "Forbes is just as strong willed as Kissa and he's in love with her. I've know Forbes for over ten years. When he gets his mind set on something, he's not going to give up. In all of the years he has worked for the Bureau, Forbes never challenged my authority until this case."

"You really think I believe that? Forbes doesn't love Kissa. He's still using her."

Africa gasped when Zane wrapped his hand around her arm and jerked her towards his muscular frame. "Forbes doesn't love Kissa. He's in love with her and I don't appreciate you insinuating that I'm a liar."

"Let go of my arm," Africa hissed as her heart sped up at Zane's closeness. It was wrong for a man to have eyes as green as his.

"Why? Is it bothering you that I'm this close?" Zane asked pulling her even closer. "I know that you're attracted to me."

Fire shot from Africa's black eyes as she glared at Zane. "You don't know what you're talking about. I can't stand you. You're a hundred times worse than Forbes."

"Prove it," Zane challenged as his eyes dropped down to her mouth then back up to her face.

"Prove what?"

"That you aren't attracted to me."

"I don't have to do anything of the sort. I told you to let go of me." Africa twisted her body, but it pressed her more into the hardness of Zane's chest. "Why can't you take no for an answer?"

"I'm like Forbes. When I see something that I like, I keep going after until I win it over."

"I'm not a prize to be won," she snapped still trying to fight off her attraction to the man holding her.

"Maybe I think you are," Zane whispered before he kissed her.

The kiss only lasted a second or two but it shook Africa, making her want more, but Zane moved away before she got what she wanted. Licking his lips, he stared down at her. "I think someone is in deep denial." Taking a card out of his pocket, he slipped it in her cleavage. "Call me when you're ready to act of those feelings." Zane gave her another quick kiss then strolled away.

"I'm never going to call you," Africa yelled after Zane. She just hoped she would be able to keep her word.

Chapter Nineteen

Dru stood shell shocked as Luke told Brad her secret. She felt as if the ground had opened up and swallowed her whole. What was she going to go? Brad knew her deepest secret now. Sure she had flirted back with him in the office, but that was different from him knowing that she was in love with him.

"How could you tell him?" she whispered glaring at her cousin. "I told you that in confidence and you just blurted it out."

"I'm sorry. I didn't mean for it to happen, but he was acting all crazy about the ring and it came out," Luke apologized. "He was bound to find out anyway."

"No, he wasn't because I was never going to tell him," she shouted slapping her cousin in the chest.

"Why weren't you going to tell me that you loved me?" Brad asked.

"It doesn't matter now," Dru muttered embarrassed.

"Yes, it does matter. I want to know."

Dru hated being put on the spot like this. It wasn't fair to her. Brad wasn't ever supposed to find out about her feelings. She was just going to turn in her resignation and move away from him and anything she felt for her boss. Now, because of her cousin's big mouth, it was all out in the open.

"I wasn't going to tell you because I know you aren't in love with me. You might find me attractive or even lust after me a little. But I'm not stupid even to believe that you're in love with me," she sighed.

"Dru, I've so much to tell you. Will you come with me so we can talk?" Brad reached for her but she moved away from him.

"No, we don't have anything to say to each other."

"Yes we do," Brad growled. "Please let me take you somewhere so we can get things out in the open."

Dru blinked back the tears in her eyes. Brad was going to try to be nice about her feelings, but she couldn't stand seeing the pity in his eyes. "Brad, I'm not going anywhere with you." She stole a glance at her cousin. "Bianca will love that ring. I hope you decide to propose to her."

"Dru, I'm really sorry. I truly didn't mean to let that slip."

"It's okay." She sighed then looked at Brad. "I'm taking the rest of the day off. I want some time to myself." Spinning on her heel, she headed back in the direction of her car.

"How's the book coming along? Are you almost finished?"

Kissa hit the keys to save her book on the laptop then looked up at the person standing in front of her. She had decided to come to the park today, so she could work on her book without getting bothered and yet here someone was in her personal space.

"Agent Rogets, how may I help you?"

"May I have a seat?" he asked pointing to the empty park beach.

"If I was to say no would you leave?"

"No, I won't," Zane replied.

"Then by all means, have a seat and ruin the rest of my day," Kissa muttered waving to the empty spot beside her.

"Thank you."

"So, what do I owe this pleasure? Are you coming to arrest one of my friends now and you need my help?" she asked sarcastically.

"With that sharp tongue of yours, I don't know why Forbes loves you," Zane complained. "I told him not to get in too deep when it came to you. I knew you would be trouble."

Kissa wasn't about to get into an argument with Agent Rogets about Forbes. The deadline for her book was fast approaching and she didn't want to ask for an extension. Brad and Dru were a wonderful couple and need their happily ever after to mean something.

"Why are you here?"

"Why do you think I'm here?" he countered.

"I think Forbes sent you here. He wants me to forgive him and he's pulling out all the stops. What can you tell me that I haven't already heard?" she complained. "I'm through with Agent Huntington and it's best you tell him that."

"I don't believe you."

"Why not?" Kissa questioned.

"Because if you hated him, you would never have let me sit down," Zane replied. "Miss Collins, Forbes really does care about you. He's about to go on another assignment and I think you should talk to him before he leaves. His focus isn't where it should be and that could get him killed."

Kissa shoved her computer back into the bag and stood up. "I'm sorry Agent Rogets, but I can't help you. Agent Huntington isn't a part of my life anymore. I know what my Uncle Thomas did was wrong, but Forbes didn't have to use me as bait to get him. I can't get over that."

Zane got up from the bench and slid his hands into the front pockets of his suit. "You need to forgive him or you're going to miss out having an amazing man in your life."

"I'm sorry, it isn't going to happen."

"Miss Collins, I really wish there was something I could say that would make you change your mind. Haven't you ever done anything before that you regretted later?"

"Yes, I allowed myself to fall in love with Forbes Huntington before I knew what kind of man that he really was," she snapped. "Now if you'll excuse me, I have to find a new place to work on my book. It's gotten a little crowded here."

Kissa walked away from Zane trying her best not to ask about Forbes and where he would be going on his next assignment. She didn't want to care about him, but she couldn't fight her emotions. As much as she wanted to deny it, Forbes meant a lot more to her than she was admitting to anyone.

"I have to clear my head. I can't stay here with everyone talking about Forbes at every turn." She didn't know where she was going to go, just that she had to get away from here for a week or two and figure out how to move on without Forbes in her life.

"You can't run away from your problems," Africa complained watching Kissa as she packed her bags for her trip. "Didn't Forbes tell you that he was leaving soon, so why do you need to leave too?"

"There are too many distractions here for me," Kissa said shoving a pink t-shirt inside her suitcase. "I want some peace and quiet so I can finish this book. Why aren't you on my side?"

"I am on your side. Aren't I allowing you to use my penthouse to stay in while you think things through?"

"You're letting me use your penthouse because you abandoned me at the book signing for Zane. I still can't believe you let him kiss you. God, that guy is such an asshole."

"I don't think Zane is all that bad," Africa retorted handing her make-up bag. "He was only trying to help get you and Forbes back together."

Pressing the make-up bag against her chest Kissa studied her agent. Africa hadn't been the same since Forbes and Zane came into their lives. Was Africa hiding something from her? Did her friend have feelings for Zane?

"You like him, don't you?" she asked waiting for a reaction.

Africa brushed an imaginary piece of lint off her sleeve. "I don't know what you're talking about. Agent Rogets and I don't have anything going on. I've spoken with him a couple of times and that's it."

"Deny it all you want to Africa, but I know you and you have feelings for Zane," Kissa laughed tossing her case into the suitcase. "I can't believe it. I'm having problems with Forbes and you're falling for his boss. Can my life get any worse?"

"Come on, are you still really mad at Forbes for arresting Thomas, or are you upset by the fact your uncle was a criminal and you didn't know it?" Africa challenged. "It has to be one or the other, but it can't be both."

She hated when Africa pushed her into a corner like this. Damn it! She wasn't ready to figure out which situation distressed her more. "I don't know. That's another reason why I have to leave for a while. I need to sort things out."

"Are you going to see Forbes before you go?"

Slamming her suitcase shut Kissa dragged it off the bed and set it by her bedroom door. A part of her did want to sneak away without laying eyes on Forbes, while another part of her did want to see him before she left.

"I'm torn," Kissa muttered falling down into a chair. "I've so much going on in my head right now. I don't have room for anything else."

Squatting down in front of her, Africa grabbed her hands. "Listen, you go on the trip and find yourself. Don't worry about the deadline for this book. I want you to focus on you and nothing else."

"I'm on a deadline."

"Let me deal with the publisher. With the way your last book is selling, I don't think they'll care about pushing back the deadline," Africa told her standing back up.

"Are you sure? I know how much the fans are waiting for Dru and Brad's story. Several fans asked about it at the book signing and I told them I was working on it." Kissa stood up and looked around the room making sure that she had everything she needed for her trip.

"I'm positive. Now grab that suitcase and get out of here. I'll lock the place up and check on it while you're gone."

"Are you sure that I can trust you?" she asked going over to her suitcase by the door. Picking it up, she looked back over at Africa. "Don't throw any wild parties while I'm gone or have sex in my bed."

"I promise that I won't have sex in your bed," Africa grinned.

"What about the other one?"

"I don't know...I love a good party."

"Stop joking around and walk me to my front door," Kissa sighed leaving her bedroom.

"I'll do better than that. I'll walk your crazy ass to your car," Africa laughed following her out the door.

Outside in her driveway Kissa paused in front of her car and against her will, thoughts of Forbes entered her mind. "I guess he didn't want to see me before he left," she mumbled getting inside her car slamming the door closed.

"Honey...you can't have it both ways. You told him not to come and then you get mad when he listens to you."

Leaning out the car window Kissa glared at Africa. "You're supposed to be my sounding board and listen to anything that I've to say. I can't help it if I wanted to see him before I left. He told me that he loved me, but he couldn't spare a few minutes to even say goodbye," she complained moving back inside the car and started it up.

"Bri, I don't know what I'm going to do with you. Why don't you catch your flight and take this time to figure things out? I know when you come back that your mind should be much clearer."

"I hate it when you're right," Kissa complained starting the car. "I'll call you when I get to the penthouse. I mean it, stay out of trouble."

Ebony eyes grew wide as a smile tipped the corners of Africa's pouty lips. "I promise that I won't do anything that will make you ashamed of me."

"Lord...I'm scared to even know what your mind is thinking," Kissa muttered as she pulled out of her driveway for the airport.

"Ma'am, I'm sorry about the delay, but I can't do anything about it. There are two other planes experiencing the same thing. You just have to wait until the plane is ready to take off," the woman told her behind the counter.

"Do you know how long the wait will be?" Kissa inquired. This is why she hated flying.

"No, I don't but I'm sure you won't be here that long," the words were said with a practiced smile.

"Thank you." Moving away from the counter Kissa walked around the airport until she found a seat over near a corner where she could be alone. She didn't feel like making chit chat with the other stranded passengers.

Settling into her seat, she dropped her head into her hands and slowly counted to ten, praying she wouldn't have to be here until her hair turned gray. Why didn't she just make a road trip out of it and drive instead? There was no way this day could get any worse for her.

"Hello, Kissa," a rich voice whispered in front of her sending her body on full alert.

No, it couldn't be.

Lifting her head, Kissa locked eyes with the gray-eyed devil that she was trying so hard to forget. What in the world was he doing here? Had Africa sent him after her? Why was she so excited to see him? No...she wasn't supposed to be feeling like this. Forbes had hurt her...it wasn't time to wonder if he still tasted the same. God, why did he smell so good? Was it because she hadn't seen him in almost two weeks?

"What are you doing here?"

"I could ask you the same question," he tossed back falling into the seat next to her.

"Did Africa send you here after me? I told her to stay out of my personal life."

Kissa leaned back in her seat and stared at Forbes. He honestly was one of the best looking men she had ever laid eyes on. Today he was wearing a black shirt with matching slacks and his hair was brushed back off his forehead. It looked a little longer than the last time she laid eyes on him. The five o'clock shadow she loved so much was still there teasing her to touch it.

"I haven't spoken to Africa in a while," Forbes replied staring back at her.

"Okay...you aren't answering my questions," she sighed frustrated. "Anyway, I don't why I'm wasting my time talking to you anyway. All you're going to do is lie to me." She jumped up from her seat only to have Forbes pull her back down.

"Baby, please don't leave. I want to talk to you," Forbes pleaded.

Jerking her arm away, Kissa glared at Forbes. "You don't have the right to touch me."

"Fine, I won't touch you," Forbes held up his hand and slid away from her. "But will you stay here and talk to me?"

"Do we really have anything else left to say to each other? Didn't we get it all out at my book signing?"

"No, we didn't get it all out. I love you and I want you to give me another chance to prove it," he practically shouted at her. "Damn it, woman! I've never been in love like this before. You're everything to me and you blowing me off like I was some one night stand that you can't get rid of."

"Kissa, I'm sorry about what happened at your house, but you can't keep blaming me for that. It's my job to bring criminals to justice and unfortunately your uncle was a criminal."

"You ruined the childhood memories I cherished the most of my uncle. I always thought it was so cool when he came to visit and had all the coolest toys for me. Do you know how it feels now to know they all came from stolen money?" Kissa accused holding her tears at bay. "He was the only family I had and now he's locked away for the rest of his life."

"I can be your family," Forbes whispered tracing her jaw with his finger. "We can make our own memories. Baby, I love you more than the air I breathe. All I think about is how you smell early in the morning. Or the way you slept on my chest after we made love. Can't you see that we're meant to be?"

"Forbes, don't," Kissa murmured as she tried to move her head away.

"I can't help it," he rasped sliding his hand into her hair. "You're everything that I want in a wife and the mother of my children. Children that I don't want to have with any other woman but you." Leaning closer he kissed her softly on the lips. Forbes moved back and trailed his thumb over her bottom lip. "I'm going away for a while, but I want you think about what I said. Do you still have the ring I gave you?" he asked looking down at her bare hand.

"Yes...I keep it in my purse," Kissa confessed. Why was she allowing Forbes to talk to her like this?

"Anytime you doubt my sincerity or love for you, look at that ring. When I gave it to you, I was Forbes Huntington...not Agent Huntington. I'm in love with you and if you never love me back, I'll never stop caring about you."

"Please stop," she whispered trying to shake off Forbes spell. "I don't need this. I'm going on a trip to clear my head and you aren't helping me."

"Where are you going?"

"I can't tell you."

"Are you going to be with another man?" Forbes growled deep in his throat. "I don't share what's mine."

Kissa thought about lying thinking it might scare Forbes off, but she changed her mind. "No, I'm going away by myself. Anyway if I was going to be with a man it wouldn't have been any of your business," she snapped.

"Oh, that's where you're wrong," Forbes corrected. "Once you shared that sweet body of yours with me, it became mine and mine alone."

Hot shivers of desire shot through her body as she remembered how it felt to make love with Forbes. He was the best she had ever been with. Forbes knew how to make each part of her body sing with pleasure.

Shaking off the memory, she quickly stood up and grabbed her bag off the floor. "Why did you have to say that to me? You know that we aren't together anymore."

Forbes stood up and pushed his hands deep into his pockets. "We're still a couple. You're only upset with me at the moment, so I'm going to leave you alone. But not forever, so this is fair warning when I come back for you...and I will come back for you...I'm not giving up until you're my wife." He spun and was gone.

Kissa opened her mouth to yell after Forbes then stopped. "I can't. I'm not ready yet," she mused, but her heart was weakening. A small smile touched her lips at the thought of being back with Forbes.

Chapter Twenty

"I know that you sent him to that airport don't bother denying it," Kissa complained staring at the window watching the steady flow of traffic on the street.

"I swear, I didn't send Forbes to the airport. I wouldn't have done that to you," Africa swore on the other end of the phone. "But how did it feel to see him again?"

Spinning around, Kissa moved around the living room and tried to forget how good it felt to have Forbes that close to her again. He had brought back so many memories that she wanted to forget. "I felt nothing at all," she lied. "It was like talking to a stranger."

"Stop lying, you know that you loved every minute of it," Africa laughed on the other end of the phone. "You're still in love with him, so why don't you stop fighting it?"

"I'm not in love with Agent Huntington. I wish you would stop saying things like that. He's in my past and that is where he's going to stay forever."

"Do you believe those lies you're telling yourself? Because I know that I don't believe them."

"I'm not lying," Kissa denied. "I mean every word that's coming out of my mouth. Forbes is out of my life and I hope that he stays out."

"Are you saying that if Forbes never crosses your path again that you won't miss him at all?" Africa challenged. "That your heart doesn't speed up every time he walks into the room, or you can't stop thinking about him at every turn?"

Kissa's wide smile spread from ear to ear and she was so happy that Africa couldn't see her face right now. "I don't think that we're talking about me anymore. Sounds like you're referring how you feel when Zane is around you."

"Zane isn't all that bad, but he does have a way," Africa laughed.

"I still can't believe you actually have a crush on one of the men that help put my uncle away," Kissa's disappointment rung out over the phone.

"Kissa, let it go. Isn't that one of the reasons you went to the penthouse? You wanted a neutral space to clear your head?"

"How can I clear my head when my best friend is falling for the enemy?" she complained hurt in her voice.

"People who live in glass house shouldn't..."

"I'm not being a hypocrite," she denied. Why would Africa say something like that to her?

"Come on. You know that you're in love with Forbes and you're too stubborn to admit it. Give the guy a second chance. Hell, at least let him take you to dinner when he gets back in town."

She knew that Africa was right. Forbes wasn't the villain she first made him out to be. Her Uncle Thomas did break the law and deserved any jail time he received, but it just hurt that the man she was in love with had to be the one that did it.

"Why are you doing this to me? I don't want to forgive him. Can't I stay mad at him a little longer?" she asked matter-of-factly. "He'll think that what he said to me at the airport is what won me over."

"Bri, Forbes is gone on another assignment for a while. He doesn't know how you're feeling. Take this time to rest and get stuff done. You'll have plenty of time to talk to him when he gets back. I know that he'll be more than happy to hear anything you've to say to him."

"When did you become such a romantic? I thought you didn't like Forbes anyway. Now you're pushing me towards him with no questions asked. Does Zane have anything to do with your sudden change of heart?"

"We aren't talking about Zane, so stop pushing the conversation over to me. You still want Forbes and don't want to admit it," Africa said.

Kissa was trying her best to fight what she knew was impossible to fight. She did want Forbes and she was willing to work things out with him. It might take them a little longer than he thought, but in time she knew that they could get back the love she first felt with him.

"I'll admit what I'm feeling if you confess that you're interested in the aloof Zane Rogets," she challenged knowing Africa would hate her for it.

"You know that I hate you, right?"

"I love you too, Africa."

"Fine, I think that Agent Rogets is very attractive, but he is a little too cocky for my tastes sometimes," Africa admitted.

"Okay...my turn. I think Forbes is one of the hottest men I've ever laid eyes on and I think that I still love him."

"You think?"

Just from the tone of her voice Kissa knew Africa was making a face at her. "I'm not saying anymore than that. This trip was supposed to be about me and nothing else, so I'm going to hang up now."

"Bye, Kissa."

"Bye, Africa."

Hanging up the phone Kissa grabbed her laptop off the living room table and headed into the kitchen. Falling down into a chair, she folded a leg in the seat and started to type.

"Why are you always running from me?" Brad asked wrapping his hand around her arm spinning her back around to face him. "You never stay still long enough for me to talk to you."

"Brad, we have nothing to say to each her."

"I think we need to talk about what your cousin told me back there. Are you really in love with me?"

"Luke doesn't know what he's talking about," she said staring down at her arm then back up to Brad's face. "Would you please let go of my arm?"

"Dru, I only want to talk to you," he sighed releasing her. "Can't you spare me a few minutes?"

"You've five minutes," she sighed looking down at her watch then back at the man she was in love with. Why couldn't she have fallen in love with the average Joe from the mail room instead of the GQ cover model standing in front of her? Brad was better looking than George Clooney and better looking than Gerald Butler on a good day.

Brad saw the way Dru was looking at him and he wasn't getting a good feeling from it. All he wanted to do was love her for the rest of his life but she was acting like she hated the sight of him.

"Can't we go somewhere more private?" he asked looking around the empty parking lot. "I don't want us talking out here in the open."

"Where do you suggest that we go?"

"How about my house?" he suggested. "I know how much you love sitting on the floor in front of the fireplace."

"I don't think so...I think right here is fine."

"Dru, please don't do this to me. You know that I only live two blocks from here. You can follow me in your car," Brad pleaded touching her lightly. "I swear I'm not going to pressure you into anything. I only want a chance to talk to you...really talk to you."

Why did she have to be so weak when it came to Brad? He had to get all sweet on her knowing that it would make her change her mind. "You won't try to make me stay longer when I want to leave?" Dru questioned already feeling herself giving in.

"I swear, I won't put any added pressure on you. Does that mean you're going to come with me?"

"I'll follow you in my car because I've to meet Neil in an hour."

Jealousy raced through his body at the sound of another man's name coming from Dru's lips. Who in the hell was Neil? Why was Dru going to blow him off to see another man? "Who is Neil? Where did you meet him? Does he mean something to you?"

"Brad, we aren't in a relationship and you have no right to ask me questions about my personal life." Turning away from him Dru headed back to her car. "Let's go. I don't want to miss my dinner date with Neil."

Biting back another question, Brad stomped to his car and got inside. He would get Dru to tell him everything that was going on between her and Neil once he got her alone. He pulled out of the parking lot and made sure that Dru was behind him as he drove towards his house. All he could think about on the drive was that Dru had fallen in love with another man and didn't want him anymore.

Why hadn't he told her weeks ago how he felt about her? Now when he was ready to admit his feelings, she was with another man and his chance of being with her was now over.

Parking inside his driveway Brad got out of his car and waited for Dru as she got out of her car. "I'm glad that you decided to come," he said when she met him by his front door. "I hope we can get everything out in the open."

"I do too, because I don't want any tension between us at work." Dru agreed stopping in front of him.

"Some tension is good, isn't it?" he asked.

"Yes, it is. However, the tension we have is bad and we need to work through it, so we can have a good working relationship. I love my job and I don't want to give a two weeks' notice."

She couldn't leave him, Brad thought in a panic. He would be lost without her in his life. "Why don't we go inside and see what we can work out?"

"Don't try to change my mind because you won't be able to. I'm not working for you anymore," she reminded him walking in front of him. "It couldn't make for a good working environment for either of us. We are now going in different directions with our lives."

Sliding past the sweetness he has grown to know and love as Dru, Brad unlocked the front door waving her inside. Once they were inside he closed and locked the door behind them. He wasn't about to let her leave to meet another man until they settled a few things between them, such as she was his and he wasn't about to let her disappear out of his life without a fight.

"Can I get you something?" he asked standing beside Dru.

"No. I'm fine. I just think we need to get this conversation over so I can leave," she replied moving away from him. "I still don't see why we couldn't have this conversation at the park instead of your house."

Resuming his spot behind Dru, Brad placed his hands on her shoulders, massaging her tense muscles. "I like to have privacy when I'm with my woman. I don't want anyone hearing what I've to say."

"I'm not your woman," Dru corrected him brushing off his touch. "I'm your employee and that's it. It will never go any further because I'm leaving."

Brad realized that he wasn't getting anywhere this away with Dru so he tried a different approach. "Tell me where you going? Have you already gotten a new job lined up this fast?" He knew that Dru was good at her job, but there was no way she had a job this quickly.

Dru took a seat on his couch and studied him. "I'm running several possibilities through my head at the moment, but I'm not quite sure where I'm going. I might take a month or two off and go back home. I haven't seen my mother in a while."

Brad dropped into a seat far enough away from Dru not to make her nervous, but it was close enough that he could touch her if he wanted to. "How is your mother? She's such a wonderful woman. I love a chance to meet her."

"She's doing well," she replied. "My mother still misses my dad, but she's doing better each and every day."

"I still don't understand why you didn't let me accompany you to the funeral. I wanted to go with you. I know that you needed someone there for you." He was still hurt that Dru didn't want him around her when he thought she needed him the most.

"Brad, you already had other appointments lined up for those three days; besides it would've looked strange if you had closed down your business for me."

"You truly don't believe me, do you?" Brad questioned leaning forward in his seat.

"Believe what?"

"That I'm madly in love with you. I have been since I first laid eyes on you in the interview." he responded with obvious love in voice.

Kissa read over the next chapter one more time, making sure that it evoked the emotions she wished for her two favorite characters. A small part of her saw herself and Forbes in Dru and Brad. Dru was fighting so hard to be apart from Brad, yet he was fighting even harder for them to be together. Brad wasn't about to give up on his love for Dru and he only wished she saw it the same way he saw her each and every time they were together.

Closing the laptop, she dropped her head down into her hands and thought about her relationship with Forbes. He swept into her life out of the blue and she fell hard for him the second their eyes connected. Every inch of his perfect body pushed her harder to learn more and what she found out was all lies.

Would she be able to come back from the way he manipulated her mind and emotions? Was she taking this too seriously by not talking things out with Forbes? Uncle Thomas had been running from the law for years and he finally got caught. His crimes didn't reflect on what kind of person she was or how she should live her life.

"Forbes, are you the man I've been writing about for most of my life? Could I have my happy ever after with you?" Kissa didn't know what to do; she was more confused now than she had been when all of this first happened.

"I want to forgive him and make everything the way it used to be, but I don't know if I can trust Forbes not to lie to me again about something important. How can I love him without trust? Don't the two go hand in hand?"

Groaning Kissa got up from the seat and found her car keys. She wasn't about to waste all her of vacation in New York worrying about Forbes. She would eventually figure out what to do when it came to him.

Chapter Twenty One

"You can't keep thinking about her or you aren't going to be able to do this job. Stone is very dangerous and if he even thinks that you're a federal agent, he'll kill you."

Forbes shoved his sunglasses down on his nose and relaxed in the warm sun of Oregon. He wasn't worry about Stone finding out his true identity. Right now, his new boss was too busy fucking two women to even care about what day it was.

"Why are you here? Aren't you supposed to be hunting after Africa? I heard that she tossed you to the side last week. Were you not the type of man she was looking for?"

"Keep it up and see if I grant you the leave of absence that you requested last week. Africa and I aren't seeing each other. We are only friends," Zane informed him a cool tone. "I'm not going to let a woman wrap me around her finger the way Kissa has done you."

"Kissa is the woman that I'm madly in love with. She has the right to have me wrapped around her finger," Forbes corrected calmly. "When you finally fall in love you'll be spouting the same stuff that I am."

"I think that's a long way down the road. Now, let's talk about Stone and this marijuana drop. Do you know when it's going to happen? Does he really have ties to the KKK?"

Forbes looked around the deserted area and he didn't see anyone, but he got a very bad feeling that he and Zane weren't alone. He couldn't put make out where it was coming from, however he got a sneaky suspicion that he might have been followed.

"Are you sure no one followed you from the airport?" he questioned sitting inside the rental car in the parking lot.

"I'm positive. I took every false turn that I could to shake someone," Zane answered staring at him. "What's wrong?"

He shrugged one large shoulder. "I'm not sure."

"You're the best in your field. Tell me what's up? You wouldn't have said anything if you weren't positive that something was off."

"I think someone is watching us, but I can't be for sure. I know that most of Stone's guards are waiting for the shipment to come in and the rest are back at the home guarding him. I got the day off because I prevented him from getting shot last night. By the way, tell Jones that he almost hit me."

"Jones thought you might enjoy the extra excitement. We wanted Stone to believe your cover and it worked," Zane stated. "Do you know how hard it was to get Stone to each approach you? The Bureau had almost giving up hope that he would take the bait."

Forbes shoved his sunglasses on top of his head and looked through the windshield. He was still getting an uneasy feeling in the pit of his stomach. Something wasn't right, but he couldn't put his finger on it.

Taking a glance at Zane he pushed his paranoia to the back of his mind. Zane was right, if he didn't get his thoughts straight Stone would catch him at a weak moment. "It almost worked a little too well. I'm glad Stone believes in bullet proof vests for his men," Forbes laughed humorlessly, "or I might not be here to find out if Kissa is the woman I think she is."

"You're actually going to give up a fifteen year career on a maybe?" Zane questioned disbelief in his voice. "What is she finds another man while you're away?"

Gray eyes turned the color of cold steel. Kissa was his and another man's hands better not touch any part of her perfect body. Surely she couldn't forget the conversation they shared back at the airport. He was holding back to give her additional time to think, but his pursuit of Kissa hadn't stopped and it wouldn't until she was his wife.

"She isn't going to do that," he bit out.

"Why are you so sure? Did she make you any promises to stay faithful? I thought she told you to stay out of her life."

Zane never had anything good to say about Kissa. All he did was find a way to point out her flaws or lack of faith in him. Shit, wasn't Zane supposed to be his best friend? When would he see that Kissa was the woman he had waited all of these years to settle down with a start a family?

"You don't like her, do you?" Forbes asked trying to see his friend point of view.

"I think Kissa is a nice woman, but I'm not positive she's the one for you. How can you give up everything you've worked so hard for to be with her?"

"I'm in love and I'm willing to give up what I've to be with Kissa. I have a dangerous job and I don't want her at home worrying about me. What if one day a suspect wants to get revenge on me by hurting her? I wouldn't be able to handle that."

Drumming his fingers on the steering wheel, Zane nodded slowly, as if his emotions for Kissa were finally getting through his friend's thick head. "I understand. As much as I'm trying to deny it, I'm starting to have deeper feelings for Africa. Just the way she argues with me is a turn-on. But I don't know if I could give it everything to be with her like you're doing."

"You'll do it," Forbes stated without hesitation

"How can you be so sure?"

"I was like you. I thought the F.B.I. was my life until I met Kissa and everything else fell into the background. She became my main focus and concern. The day she yelled at me to stay out of her life about ripped my heart apart. I wasn't prepared for her anger it almost knocked me off my feet."

"After I'm finished with Stone, nothing is going to stand in my way for reaching Kissa. She's on a little vacation now, but when I go, I'll claim her as mine forever. Ms Kissa Collins isn't going to know what hit her."

"I wouldn't get overly confident if I were you. She's one tough lady," Zane stated in a cool tone then started the car. "I believe you might have to give her more than a few kisses and flowers."

"I'm dying to give her what I know we need and Kissa isn't going to be able to fight it either." Forbes' voice held a hint of a challenge.

Forbes pulled out onto the highway and drove back in the direction that he left his car. Stone's men were good and he didn't want to take any chances that his car might have been bugged. This assignment was making him nervous because he couldn't read his new boss. Stone was like a roller coaster; he wasn't quite sure in what direction he was going to turn in any given moment.

"Don't drop me off by my car. Let me off at the corner and I'll walk the rest of the way." Forbes glanced back over his shoulder out the rear window. "I still get the feeling someone is following me, but I haven't seen anyone all day."

"Do you think you're pushing yourself too hard on this case? I can always pull you out if it gets too hot for you," Zane suggested.

"No...I can handle whatever is coming my way. It's probably just my mind playing tricks on me. It has been a while since I was undercover on a case like this. Stone isn't a man that likes to be messed with. I've seen him do things that I couldn't do anything to stop it."

"Do you think we can use it against him once we arrest him?" Zane parked by his car in the park. "We need all the evidence that we can get against that SOB. He's one mean bastard. There's about six pages in his file about what he tried to do to his parents."

"I know, I read that." Forbes still shivered at the words and images that reading Stone's file placed in his mind. He wouldn't be able to handle it if someone like that psycho got his hands on Kissa.

"It was a blessing that his sister came home early from cheerleading practice and stopped him before he could do any real damage," Zane explained. "He was one sick little kid and all of that information is hidden on him. If I didn't have a friend in a high place, we would have never gotten our hands on it."

"I was just thinking I would kill him with my bare hands if he even thought about Kissa. We have to bring him down. I don't want someone like that running around free on the streets." The venom in Forbes' voice shocked the man next to him.

"Don't worry, we'll get him behind bars. You won't have to be under much longer. All we need is Stone videotaped selling the drugs and guns. Can you set that up for us?"

"Didn't I work my way up to his right hand man in only a matter of weeks? It won't be a problem to take him with the drugs and guns." It would be a piece of cake since Stone loved bragging about both.

"Being Stone London's right hand henchman and him freely selling guns and drugs with me standing there is a different matter. He's good at what his does and that's why he has been on the F.B.I.'s most wanted list now for over five years," Forbes said.

"You're top in your field. The Bureau knows that you can get this psycho off the street and he's feeling the heat. Why do you think we picked you? When the time comes we know that there will be ice water in your veins."

"I'm tired of having that image. I want to be a family man with the house and dog to come home to. I've grown weary of watching my back all the time wondering is someone after me," Forbes sighed massaging the side of his temple with his fingertips. "Do you how hard it was not to follow Kissa? I watched her get on the plane with envy at her having some free time without me."

"Kissa'd better be worth all the agony that you're putting yourself through. I think she's very pretty with that girl next door image, but can you really stay faithful to her?" Zane questioned. "I haven't forgotten all the hot women that used to fall at your feet at the office."

Dropping his hand Forbes moved his head pinning his friend with a silencing look. "First, don't look at my woman. You don't have the right to determine if I can be faithful to her or not. Kissa is mine and I'm not about to share her with anyone else." He hoped that his friend finally understood him because he was getting tired of repeating himself.

"Secondly, the women from our job know the score and that's why I dated so many of them. They knew our relationship wasn't on an emotional level, but only for sex and nothing else. Don't ever place Kissa in the same category as them." The threat hummed in his voice and Forbes knew Zane caught it.

"You know, the only reason I allow you to talk to me like that is because we're friends and other bosses would have fired your ass by now."

"I know, that's why I do it," Forbes replied opening the car door. "I won't be able to make contact again for about two weeks, but I'll wear my watch at all times so you can track me." Getting out of the car, he slammed the door closed. "Be careful, I'm still getting this strange feeling we're being watched."

"Do you want to come back with me? I don't want you to stay here if you don't feel comfortable. Kissa already doesn't like me. She'll kill me if something happens to you."

Moving back from the vehicle Forbes waved Zane off. "No, I can handle myself. You know that. Stone needs to be brought down and I'm just the man to do it. It shouldn't take too much longer and then I'm out of here."

"Okay, but don't hesitate to make a phone call if you need to." Zane gave him a thumb's up sign then drove off his car blending easily into the heavy afternoon traffic.

Forbes quickly made his way over to his car and got in. He didn't want Stone to wonder where he'd been for the past two hours. His new mark was more than a little paranoid and the slightest things set him off. Pulling out of the parking lot he turned in the opposite direction of Zane going back to his job, but with thoughts of Kissa on his mind.

Chapter Twenty Two

"Jacob, did you get everything you need done while you were out? I thought I might have to send B.J. after you." Stone's voice carried from across the room hitting him the second he walked through the door. Forbes still wasn't used to being addressed with his fake identity yet.

"Yes, I got a lot done. Thanks for giving me the extra two hours off. It was a huge help," he answered shaking his head at the drink Stone offered him.

"I've never known a man that didn't like a good whiskey," Stone commented taking a sip of the dark liquor.

"My old man beat me and my mother every day because he loved the taste of that stuff. I promised my mother that I would never touch it."

"I like a man that respects his mother and knows how to keep his word. It shows his character and I can trust his actions when the time comes." Stone downed the last of his drink and placed the glass on the shiny surface of the bar. "I had some time to think while you were gone and I've come to a decision."

Keep your cool. This may be what Zane and I've been waiting for. "Are you going to fire me after I saved your life?" he joked but inside his heart was beating a mile a minute. Stone London wasn't a man to be messed with. If he wanted you to go missing and not be found, he had the power to make it happen with his connections to the KKK and other groups.

"On the contrary, I want to give you a promotion. I like your look and your ability to handle yourself in a difficult situation, but you have to pass a test first."

He didn't like the sound of this at all. "What kind of test? I hope it doesn't involve math because I might as well as drop out now," Forbes joked again hoping to break the tension he felt building. Would he have enough time to warn Zane about this?

Stone's chuckle sent a flicker of apprehension through his body. Even the man's laugh was evil and very disturbing. "A man with jokes. I think I'm beginning to like you more and more. However, if you ever cross me, you'll regret the day you were born."

If Stone was trying to draw a response from him, then he wasn't going to get the one he wanted. "A lot of men have crossed me in the past and lived to regret it to. I'm not a man to be played with either. I take my job very seriously."

"That's good to know because the last man who tried to befriend me turned out to be an undercover cop and let's just say that my men paid his wife a little visit. The last time I heard about her she was still in that mental hospital."

Forbes faltered in the silence that engulfed them. He was more shaken that he cared to admit. He was so thankful that

Kissa was out of harm's way and Stone didn't have a clue about her.

"I never had any use for cops either. They were always up my ass when I was a kid. I think they're a waste of the tax payer's money," Forbes tossed in waiting for Stone's response.

Copper eyes that were usually flat and emotionless lit up with a shine that almost made him that a step back. "Fuck, I wish I had found you years ago. I needed a man like you beside me when I planned some of my attacks back in the day."

Here it is! "What kind of attacks? I love trading good stories."

There was a lethal calmness to Stone as his eyes stared into his. "Now isn't the place to go into this, but if you pass my test, I'll be more than happy to share my old stories with you, Jacob. However, I'm needed some place else, so we need to get moving."

Forbes waited while Stone picked up a black bag from the side of a chair then followed his mark out the door, worried about what his test was going to be. He had to get in touch with Zane as soon as he had a moment to himself.

"How many times have you dreamt about him over the past week? Don't say none, because I know you and you can't lie to me if you wanted to." Africa shoved the piece of baked bread into her mouth and waited.

"Aren't you supposed to be here to help me with the last couple of chapters of my book? I didn't think this lunch would turn into a hundred and one questions about Forbes," Kissa answered shoving her salad with grilled chicken fingers away from her. "I'm not thinking about him anymore. The phone call the other day was a lapse in judgment on my part."

"No, it was the sound of the walls of Kissa finally falling down. You were acting like a woman in love again and I was so proud of you. I can ask Zane to tell Forbes you want to talk to him."

"You're still talking to Zane? I thought you didn't like the standoffish agent? Is there something deeper going on? Have the two of you played hide the sausage yet?" Kissa ducked as a piece of bread flew past her head and landed with a thump on the pavement behind her.

"Play hide the sausage," Africa's voice broke into a fit of uncontrollable giggles until she finally settled down. "Can't a bestselling author come up with something better than that?"

She grinned mischievously. "I thought it was cute."

"Well, I don't think it was."

"Oh, so you want to do the bed mambo but he doesn't, is that it?"

"How did we get the conversation turned in my direction away from you?" Africa frowned.

"I think talking about you and Zane is a lot more interesting than anything I've to say about Forbes and his disappearing act." Kissa wasn't ready to admit she was actually worried about him.

"You're worried about him, aren't you?"

A momentary look of discomfort crossed Kissa's face. She was keenly aware of Africa's scrutiny. Kissa wavered, trying to comprehend what she was feeling against what she didn't want to feel for Forbes, yet her heart was winning over her mind. "Yes, I'm concerned about him," she finally confessed.

"That's good. It means there still something between the two of you. I'll see if Zane can tell me anything the next time he calls. I doubt that he will, but I can put a bug in his ear for Forbes to call you."

"I don't know."

"Bri, for once stop over thinking your life and just let it happen. I can promise you it will surprise you more than you could ever visualize."

"All right, I'll do it," Kissa sighed giving in, "but you better be right."

"When have I ever been wrong?" Africa asked then winked at her.

Chapter Twenty Three

"You don't love me. I wish you would stop telling me that. Why do you feel the need to torment me like this?" Dru hadn't considered how Brad had such power over her. His words made her body grow moist.

"I love you. Hell, why do you think I made excuses for us to work late almost every night since you started working for me? I wanted to spend every second of the day around you."

"That's called lust...not love."

"Who hurt you so damn bad that you won't give me a chance to prove my love? Was it that Neil guy you're in such a hurry to get to? How long has this relationship been going on? Where did you meet him?"

"You have no right to ask me any of those questions," Dru fired back. "How many business lunches have you engaged with that involved a gorgeous looking woman? I never asked you about them, so stay out of my business."

"I want you to ask me," Brad confessed easing closer. "I would stand outside the office door dreaming about the jealousy that would pop in those chocolate eyes of yours, but it never came."

"You actually wanted me to get upset about the women you spent time with? What good would that have done for me?"

"Dru, it would have shown me everything I've ever wanted from you. Do you realize how standoffish you come off sometimes? I fell in love with you despite it. My heartstrings get more entangled with you more and more each day."

"Stop, I can't listen to this." She tried to leave but Brad yanked her back against his solid frame.

"When are you going to stop running and let me cherish you the way I desire? Do you know that I think about the way you talk and how your beautiful lips move when you form certain words? Do you realize you have me hypnotized?"

"No."

"Good, because I wouldn't want anything to hinder me from doing this," he answered.

"Doing what?"

Brad captured her mouth in a kiss so fast that all she could do was lean into his body and let him take control. Dru thought about fighting as she usually did, however the way Brad's tongue was licking at the corner of her mouth made that thought evaporate from her mind.

Parting her lips, she raised herself to meet his hot kiss. She kissed him back with the hunger that she had been hiding for weeks, scared Brad wouldn't return her affections.

"Mine," he breathed against her lips.

"What?" she moaned still lost in the magic of the kiss.

"You taste like you belong to me and only me. I'm not going to share you with another man after a kiss like that...so Neil can go to hell."

Leaning back in Brad's arms, Dru slowly allowed his words to sink in; the harder she tried to ignore the truth, the more it persisted. Brad was the man for her, but how were they going to make things work between them? She loved her private time, but he didn't see it like that.

She pushed herself away from Brad, placing some much needed distance between them. "I can't get into this with you now. I can't be late. I need to meet with Neil. I'll call you later," Dru rushed out, hurrying from Brad's house before he could stop her.

Hitting the key strokes to save her last chapter, Kissa waited while the laptop did its thing and recalled how it felt to be with Forbes. She remembered the ecstasy of being held against his strong body and the warmth of his breath on her neck. How good his skin smelled right after he got out of the shower.

Forbes knew that he had left a burning imprint of her body and mind. It wasn't fair that he had her trapped like this. Was this how her life would be without Forbes in it? Could she really love another man the way she still loved that damn F.B.I. agent? For God's sake, she was losing sleep over him, wondering was he dead or alive.

His face popped up in her mind when she least expected it, smiling, serious, or in deep thought about something he couldn't share with her. All of those times they spent in bed together just talking about anything off the wall brought out another round of painful memories of how he used her.

But what about the stolen moments that had together outside the photo shoot or in her kitchen when Forbes gave her the ring? He was gentle and loving then, like a man who was truly in love and wanted to spend the rest of his life with her.

"I'm so confused about what I should do. I keep going back and forth with this. One minute I hate him, and in the next I would love to be wrapped in his arms again. Please God; give me a sign about what I need to do."

Standing in the back of the back of the crowded room, Forbes listened in silence as Stone sprouted his poisonous words against anyone who wasn't like him and the other hate seekers around him.

The crisp whiteness of Stone's pressed shirt stood out perfectly against his tan, setting off the pale blond of his hair. How did he find so many people in Oregon that share his hateful views? Sure the meeting was taking place on the outskirts of Oregon, but the massive crowd here tonight overwhelmed even him.

Just hearing Stone's one-sided views made his stomach turn in revulsion. He thanked God again Kissa was far away from an individual like Stone. He wouldn't think twice about killing the flame that burned bright in her eyes.

At the sound of his name being mentioned from the stage brought his attention back to what was going on. What was that scum up to now, he wondered as Stone waved him towards the front. As he strolled through the swarm of people, Forbes tried to maintain a blank expression on his face.

It wouldn't do him any good if Stone saw his true feelings reflected in his eyes. All of this was a show for one purpose and one purpose only, and that was to knock this organization down to its knees. Standing on the platform, he stood still waiting to see where Stone was going this time.

"Everyone, since my last meeting I've acquired a new member with my beliefs. I would l like to introduce my new bodyguard, Jacob. Not only is he an outstanding bodyguard, but he's willing to do anything that I ask of him without question. Men like Jacob are hard to come by."

"Let's welcome Jacob to our little family. I have very high hopes for him," Stone rattled on next to him.

"Welcome Jacob," the room uttered back like brainwashed puppets. "We're happy to have you here with us."

As the roar of applause thundered around him Forbes thought, I'll never share the same repellent opinions as you. My trigger finger is itching to put a bullet into you, but it's not quite time yet.

As the noise grew quiet Stone whispered in his ear, "Don't be shy. This is your night say something to your new family."

You don't want to know what I would really like to say. Forbes silently thought before the open his mouth and uttered. "Thank you. I'm pleased to be here with everyone tonight and listen to the wisdom of Stone. I only hope I can live up to the vision he has of me." The first chance he had, he had to call Zane and fill him in on this new development.

"Jacob, there isn't any need for you to worry. I know I can count on you and you passing your test when the time comes will only seal the deal between us." Stone grinned slapping him on the back.

Forbes tried not to flinch as the cheers continued about him as he became a part of a society that he had always hated and couldn't wait to bring down. The Bureau had been following Stone as far as he could remember and it was going to give him such satisfaction to bring down the arrogant bastard as his last assignment.

Later that night, the black clad figure kept moving until it was far away from the house, concealed in the darkness. He knew that he didn't have a lot of time, but this information had to get out and soon. Pulling the cell phone from his back pocket he dialed the number quickly. The phone rang only once before it was answered.

"I'm in," Forbes whispered. "Stone introduced me a new member of his family tonight."

"Good. Do you know anymore about this test you have to pass?" Zane asked.

"No, but it has to be coming up soon because he's very excited about me proving my loyalty to him."

"I don't like the sound of this. I hope he gives you enough time to contact me so we can get something set up. With the way his mind works, Stone could have anything in mind for you to do."

"I know...but I'll try to see if he'll tell me what it is," Forbes said. "Is there anything else that I need to know about before I go?"

"There is something, but I don't know if I should tell you."

"Is it about Kissa? Has something happened to her? Is she dating someone else?" Forbes rattled off the questions, not giving Zane a chance to answer him.

"Yes, it's about her," Zane cut in. "No, she not hurt or dating anything else that I know of. Africa left me a voice message saying that Kissa was worried about you."

Kissa was concerned about him. Forbes barely swallowed down the shout of pleasure in time. He didn't need to let anyone know that he was outside instead of his room. The guards wouldn't be on this side of the field for at least another hour. That might give him enough time to call Kissa and let her know that he was okay.

"Forbes, you can't call her tonight," Zane informed him. "We have to make sure none of the phone calls are getting tracked by Stone. Give us two days and then you can make contact with her. This is so against policy, but I know that you'll do it with or without my help."

"You know me so well, my friend. I better go and make sure no one is looking for me. I'll call Kissa on Friday from this phone. Make sure I have a secure line." He disconnected the phone and shoved it back into his back pocket. Hurrying around the corner he stopped in his tracks as Stone came out the back door.

"Jacob, I thought you were in your room. What are you doing out here?"

"I couldn't sleep so I decided to go from a walk. I've always been a night person. I feel this is the best time to clear your head and think."

"Don't lie to me," Stone said moving closer.

Hold your cool, he thought. "I'm not lying to you."

"I remember my first meeting and how hyped up I was afterwards. It's okay if you have to get out and release some of that energy."

"Sorry," Forbes apologized. "I just didn't want you to think I was crazy or something. It all just hit me so fast and I came out here to blow off some steam."

"Not a problem, but next time let one of the guards know you're leaving the house. I would hate for one of them to shoot my best bodyguard in years."

"Will do," Forbes replied.

"How about you join me for a drink?" Stone asked heading back towards the door. "I had the maid buy some non alcoholic stuff for you."

"Sounds good to me," he followed Stone back into the house and sent up a silent prayer of thanks his new boss hadn't came out looking for him five minutes earlier.

Chapter Twenty Four

Pushing the covers off her head, Kissa reached for the evil beast that wouldn't stop bothering her. She thought if she ignored the damn thing it would stop and go away, but that wasn't happening. Why couldn't she get what she wanted?

"What!" she snapped shoving the object of turmoil to the side of her face.

"I've been trying to get in touch with you for the past two days. Where have you been? Zane told me that you were worried about me. Is that true? Are you concerned about my well-being?" Forbes deep voice penetrated the sleep of her mind. Rolling over in the bed, Kissa noticed it was two thirty in the morning.

"Forbes, where are you? Why are you whispering?" Mixed feelings surged through her at the sound of his voice, but happiness won over all of them.

"I can't talk long, but I had to hear your voice. Do you know how much I love and miss you? I'm counting the days until this case is over and I can be back in your arms. Kissa, have you forgiven me yet? I need to know so I can clear my mind and focus on this creep I'm working for." His voice was steady and unsteady, as her words were going to make or break him.

Had she gotten over the rough start she experienced with Forbes to see who he was beneath the surface? Was she finally able to separate the F.B.I. agent from the man he was desperate for her to see?

"Forbes, I love you and I want you to be safe. A big piece of me would die if something happened to you. Are you sure that it's safe for you to call me?"

When Forbes spoke to her again, his voice was tender, almost a murmur, "I'm good at my job; nothing is going to happen to me. However, I need for you to promise me something then I can get more involved with this assignment."

"What is the promise?"

"Promise me that you won't ever make me wait that long to hear you say that you love me. I almost thought I had lost you," he admitted in her ear.

"Were you about to give up on me and move on to another woman?" she questioned. Kissa knew that wasn't true, but she wanted to hear Forbes say it.

"Baby, you're in my blood. There's nothing that you could ever do that would make me give up on you. I'm going to be in love with you for the rest of my life." The low and smooth sound of his voice made her think about their future and all the happiness it would entail.

"That's good to hear. Is this case hard on you? Do you know how much longer you'll be there?" Kissa understood that Forbes had to do his job, but she rather him be here in the penthouse with her. "I miss you so much."

"Honey, I can't tell you about my assignment. Just know that I'm thinking about you and when I go to sleep at night, you're the woman in my dreams."

"Have you been reading some of my romance books again?"

"No…I haven't why?" Forbes asked.

"It's nothing, but you sound like one of the men from my novels. I thought maybe you were taking pointers from them or something," she teased savoring her time with Forbes.

"Kissa, everything I'm telling you is coming from my heart. I love you and want to spend the rest of my life with you."

"Forbes, I feel the same way. I can't wait until you're home."

"I've to go, but can you do something for me first?"

"Ask anyway and I'll try my best," she replied.

"Can you call me something besides Forbes? Like sweetheart, baby, darling or an endearment that you're fond of? I'm going to use it to help me get to sleep tonight."

"Darling, I hope you have dreams filled with me tonight, because I know when I close my eyes, you're going to be in mine. I love you so much, baby."

"Forever?"

"Forever and ever," Kissa responded with all the love she had in her body and soul.

"I have to go," Forbes groaned, "but I'll call you again as soon as I get a chance. It's against policy, but when Zane said you wanted to talk to me I decided to live a little dangerously."

"Don't you dare get yourself killed because of me. When you come back to me, I want you all in one piece and walking on your two legs. Promise me," Kissa begged.

"I promise. I'll try to call again when I get a place to do it. Goodnight, Kissa."

"Good night, baby. I'm so happy you called me."

The dial tone went dead in Kissa's ear before she could utter another word to Forbes, however she was on beyond ecstatic about her phone call with him. It put her in the writing mood. Tossing the covers off her body, she climbed out of bed and headed over to her computer. Kissa wasn't seated two minutes before her fingers raced across the keyboard.

"I was really surprised when you called me. I haven't heard from you in over six months. So, what's wrong?" Neil questioned.

"Can't I invite my estranged father to lunch?" Dru answered already regretting her decision to talk to her father about her problems.

"You haven't referred to me as your father since I divorced your mother over eighteen years ago. Before the ink was dry on the paper I became Neil in your eyes. I'm just surprised you're calling me that now."

"I remember that day. Your divorce was finalized on the same day as my high school graduation. Mama cried so hard that she made herself sick. I didn't go out to any parties that night and stayed home with her."

"Dru, this past is buried. How about we leave it there? Care to tell me about the real reason you came to me and not your mother?"

"Mama isn't the reason I can't commit to a relationship, you are."

"Who do you want to commit to? Do I know this man?"

"Yes, it's my boss. Brad told me that he loved me today," she blurted out, "but I can't get involved with him."

"I've never met Brad, but the way you talked about him the few times we have met for lunch, he seemed like a man that you were falling for. Care to tell me why you don't want to let him into your life?"

"I can't put everything into him the way mama did you and we end up hating each other. I'm head over heels in love with Brad and if he finds out how much I care, he'll try to control me. He practically forbade me from coming to see you today. I'm not use to that and I don't want it in my life."

"Are you saying Brad has control issues?"

"Not necessarily, but he does love to get his way. I'm not going to be an arm piece for him and not having a say in anything I do. Brad is a wonderful guy, however he can't keep getting jealous when I talk about another man. I have my own life, hopes and dreams that I want to accomplish. Achieving some of those things might involve getting help from him."

"Tell him that," Neil interjected. "He'll understand if he really does love you."

"The same way you understood about mama waiting to live out her dreams?"

"Dru, don't go there."

"Why not? My mama had dreams that you shut down."

"Susan made her own decisions and was happy with them until I realized that I wasn't in love with her anymore. We were having problems way before your mother decided to work outside the home."

"See, that's what I'm talking about. Brad knows that I love working, but I can see him suggesting that I stay at home with the kids while he works. What if he falls out of love with me when I tell him I want to earn a living too? Right now, he's okay with me working, but he so much like you on some level that it scares me."

"Dru, Brad isn't me. You can't live in fear of the unknown. My problems with your mother shouldn't hold you back from falling in love. If Brad wants to give you the world, then let him do it."

"I shouldn't have called you," Dru grumbled under her breath. "I don't think you really understand me."

"I understand you fine, princess," Neil chuckled. "You can't get me to say what you wanted to hear and you're pissed at me."

"That isn't true," she denied.

"Yes, it is. I'm your father and I can tell when you're in pain. You're in love and it scares the hell out of you, doesn't it?"

"Fine, I am in love and I'm afraid that I might lose Brad because I'm terrified to commit to him the way he wants."

"I know I haven't been the best parent to you over the years, but don't let your childhood stand in the way of your happiness now. Go find Brad and tell him how you feel. I'm betting he'll be more than eager to prove his love."

Dru wanted to believe that so bad, but how could her father really know that would happen? "How can you be so sure?" she asked with skepticism in her voice.

"I'm a man and we love to show the woman in our life how much we care about her, especially the ones we want to make our wives."

Neil's words were starting to make her believe. Brad did care enough about her help her work through her problems. Grabbing her purse, she stood up and a small smile touched her mouth when she met her father's eyes.

"Thank you for your help." She spun away from the table and hurried from the coffee shop.

"I'm here anytime you need me, princess," Neil said as Dru raced out the door to find Brad.

Chapter Twenty Five

"How is everything going? Have you spotted any trespassers?" Stone's voice came through the tiny earpiece stuck in his ear. "I don't want anyone trying to stop the meeting. It might turn out to be the most important one of the year."

Forbes stood at the side of the building and scanned the crowd for any signs of hidden agents trying to blend in. He spotted two over at the far left but quickly turned his head so not to draw attention to them.

"No boss, I don't spot a thing. Surely, no one is dumb enough to try anything, today not with this many people here," he stated back in the mouthpiece.

"You would be surprised at how many protesters showed up last year causing all kinds of problems and ruined everything. I had to bribe some cops to keep us safe this year."

He swallowed down a curse. Well there went that idea of getting assistance from the local law enforcement if he needed it. How was he supposed to know who was and wasn't on the take when it came to Stone?

"I didn't know you had some cops on our side. You're a lot better than I thought you were. I'm very impressed. When do I get to meet these guys and just how deeply do your connections run?"

He could only envision the smug look that passed over Stone's face. This guy really had a God complex. "Oh, I've several friends in high places," Stone bragged, "but we can't talk about it now. I'm about to go on stage. Don't forget to turn the channel to a lower station. I want to continue to talk to you but without other people listening in."

"I'm going to take a walk around the grounds since you have Calvin with you. I don't want any overly nosy people sneaking inside the house."

"Good plan. Let me know instantly if you find something out of sorts." A static sound echoed in his ear as Stone changed his pack to a different frequency.

I'm not going to tell you a damn thing you bastard. All I want to do if throw your ass in jail for several years and toss away the key, he thought. He greatly despised being around someone like Stone. But he was the only guy at the Bureau that would fit in with the look that Stone wanted in his family.

Forbes stayed where he was until Stone took the stage drawing everyone's attention in his direction. The cheers and screams exploded the second Stone flashed the million dollar smile he was known for. He didn't know which was scarier the way these people flocked to him or how Stone thought of himself as some kind of hero for his race.

Slipping around the building, he strolled slowly in the direction of the old abandoned barn at the far left of the property. He couldn't chance anyone easing up on him while he took care of business. The openness of the area gave him free reign to watch for any unwanted guests trying to surprise him.

Pausing by the barn's door, he knocked twice and waited for it to open. Seconds later it cracked open enough for sound to come out, but not enough for a passerby to see anyone's face.

"You're late," Zane pointed out as if he didn't already know that.

"Sorry, I was talking to Stone and I'm glad that I did. Do you know that he has some of the local polices are in his pocket?"

"Shit, did he give you any names? I can't believe how deep this guy's ties run."

"Of course not, he trusts me with a lot. However, he's still keeping a lot of stuff from me. I'm pretty sure after I pass this test things will start looking better for me. I only wished I knew what it was going to be. I hate being left out in the dark like this."

"I know. We aren't going to have enough time to prepare for anything if he doesn't give you something to go on. Hopefully, he doesn't want you to do something to illegal like commit murder or sell drugs to an elementary school kid."

Several possibilities of what Stone might require of him had raced through his brain the last couple of days, but he wasn't sure about any of them. Stone was a chameleon. He never knew what going on in that psycho's mind.

"Do you have any plans set up to have me follow or to intervene if Stone has something sinister up his sleeve? It's eerie to hear him talk about the one perfect race and not say anything. He would shoot me dead if he knew I was in love with Kissa."

"Whatever you do, Stone can't ever know about her. We have both read the reports of what unspeakable crimes he has done to African American women in the past," Zane stressed. "Keep your wits about you and everything should be fine. Now take this."

Forbes felt something shoving him in the middle of his back. Reaching back he grabbed the sheet of piece out of Zane's hand. "What is this?" he asked slipping it into his back pocket.

"That is the new number you use to get in touch with me," Zane replied. "Just make sure you dial in the code before you dial my phone."

"Why am I getting a new number for you? Was the other number not safe?"

"Someone was trying to trace your calls, but we aren't sure if they were coming from here because they stopped before we could find the correct location. We don't want your cover blown yet so I got you a new number."

"I don't want my cover blown either. I promised Kissa that I'll come back to her." The words slipped out and instantly

Forbes recognized his mistake. Zane was going to be up in arms that he called Kissa on his cell phone.

"Please tell me that you didn't call Miss Collins on your old phone?" His boss' voice barked through the crack in the door. "We don't have the time or manpower to be protecting her if Stone finds out about her. Your phone call could have placed her in a lot of danger."

Forbes thought his heart literally stopped beating at the thought of Kissa being placed in any form of danger because of him. He had missed her and needed to hear her voice for a few minutes. "Zane, you have to check on her and make sure she's safe," he pleaded.

"I can't do that."

"Yes you can and you know it. I know that if it was Africa you would have been there the next day checking on her. Kissa is important to me and you should feel the need to protect her as much as I do. Shit man, we have been friends for over ten years. Can you do this for me?"

He spun around and faced Zane not caring if anyone from the rally saw him. "I'll leave tonight and not come back if you don't do it. You know I'm not kidding with you."

"I've told you more than once not to threaten me." Zane's voice carried a unique tone that would have most men scared, but Forbes wasn't.

"Zane, I'm not threatening you. I only suggested that you check on Kissa for me. Can you do that for me?" he asked again, and this time his voice was friendlier.

"I know that if I don't check you'll go crazy with worry, so I'll do it," Zane finally agreed. "Now get back to that meeting and get on Stone's good side. We're going to need a lot on him, because he has excellent lawyers. We can't let him get off on a technically."

"Stone isn't about to slip through the cracks again. I'll become his best friend. It's going to give me get pleasure to bring him down."

Although he didn't answer, Zane's face spoke for him. His boss wasn't going to take anymore demands from him after this. It was a good thing that he was retiring after this case or he might not have a job waiting for him.

Chapter Twenty Six

Kissa leaned against her weight against the doorframe more than a little taken back at the person standing on the other side. She had thought it was the delivery man bringing her food, but she was completely thrown by who she found.

"I can't believe your actually here. Has hell frozen over?"

"I know that we haven't been the best of friends, however I know that we both care about Forbes. He made me promise to come and check on you. He's so in love with you."

Dark eyes shined with warmth at Forbes name. A grin spilt across her face from ear to ear. "I feel the same way about him. I'm glad that I got over what I was feeling towards Forbes. He called me the other night to make sure I was doing okay."

"Forbes is a good guy. Don't ever tell him I said that or I'll deny it to the end. I'm glad he came to the Bureau. He was a wonderful addition and an even better friend."

"I'm sorry that I was being rude. Would you like to come in for a drink? My manners aren't usually this bad," Kissa laughed waving Zane in with her hand. "I swear I don't hate you as much as you think I do."

"Ms. Collins, I never thought you hated me, however I do think our strong personalities clash sometimes. Thanks for the offer, but I've to be somewhere in twenty minutes. I really only dropped by to check on you for Forbes. He was going crazy thinking about you."

She didn't need three guesses to figure out where Zane was going next. "Africa isn't at home you do know that, right? She's gone with Cameron to North Carolina."

"Who in the hell is Cameron and why has Africa gone away with him?" Zane demanded like a man falling in love. Kissa could barely keep the smile off of her face.

"He's her ex-boyfriend. They were together for about three years when he decided he wasn't ready to get married. I think he's trying to win her back."

Dark blue eyes drilled into her as Zane rattled off another question. "How long have they been gone?"

"Two…three days at the most," she shrugged. "I think she's coming back here next week instead of going back to Texas."

"Where did they go?"

"I can't tell you that. Africa promised me not to tell anyone. She wanted time to see could she work out things with him. You know how it is with your first love and all."

"Africa thinks she's in love with this guy?" Zane asked but without his usual smugness.

Guilt rode her at doing this to Zane, but Africa was away with Cameron trying to see if he was still the one for her or if she should see where things could go with the man standing in front of her.

"Why don't you go back and tell Forbes that I'm okay?" Kissa suggested. "I promise that when Africa gets back in town I'll have her call you." There wasn't anything else that she could do but that. Her mind was more focused on Forbes getting back home safe and sound to her. She had so much that she needed to tell him.

"How about you come with me?"

"Are you saying that I'm in danger?" What kind of assignment was Forbes on that would place her in danger? "Is someone after me or something?"

"No...no one is after you. I thought maybe you would like to get away from the penthouse for a while. You can bring your laptop and work on your book."

"I'm quite happy here so I'll pass, but thank you for offering. Are you sure that you don't want to come in for a drink or something to eat?" Kissa was hoping to get something out of Zane about Forbes' location once he got inside.

He shook his head. "Since Africa isn't around I should head back to the airport and try to see are there any flights available. I'm glad that you're okay. I'll tell Forbes to stop worrying about you." Zane looked at her intently for a few seconds, then strode away from her back towards the elevators at the end of the hall.

"I don't know what Africa sees in him and I really don't care as long as he brings Forbes back home in one piece," Kissa muttered going back inside the penthouse closing the door behind her.

She was halfway back to her computer when the doorbell rung again. "Lord, will I ever get any peace so I can finish this book?" Spinning back around, she went back to the door and flung it open. "Can I help you..." was all she got out before everything went black.

Chapter Twenty Seven

"Jacob, I was very impressed with you at the rally today. This was your very first one and you handled it like a pro. My past bodyguards have gotten extremely nervous at crowds smaller than that. Do you have ice water running through your veins?"

Shit! I never thought about showing some fear. "I was nervous but I didn't want to show it in front of you. I like being your right hand and I don't want anyone to take my place." Nice save, he thought.

"You have nothing to worry about. None of the guys here are in the same league as you. They are happy to stay at the position I have them in," Stone replied removing his gun from the back of his pants tossing it on the desk.

"Why do you feel the need to carry a gun if you have such confidence in my abilities to save you?" Stone wasn't packing that gun when they left the house, so where did it come from?

"Is that a present from one of your fans?" he asked nodding towards the weapon.

"As a matter of fact it was. A young woman gave it to me after I kissed her. She wanted to show me her gratitude for being who I am. Isn't that amazing? All I've to do is stand there and speak my mind and people just flock to me."

Yeah, and they'll follow you anywhere like lamb to a slaughter too. I've to end your reign of terror before innocent people get hurt. On the evil scale, Stone was in the top five percent and it sickened him that he was in any way associated with someone like him.

"Stone, if I'm not overstepping my place, how did you become involve in with Hush?" Please talk until your heart is content so I can bring down the rest of the racially prejudiced people that support you. Moving across the room, Forbes relaxed inside a plush chair that cost more than a year of his salary. "I admire a man that can take control the way you have with your family. It gives me something to work towards."

"I don't mind telling you at all. I love being the leader of Hush." Stone came over and took a seat across from him. Crossing one leg over the other, he took on a laid back position like he had all the time in the world to boast about his past crimes. "I wasn't always the leader of Hush. The first group I joined was in Tennessee and I was a member there for about three and a half years, but it broke up after too many fights within the organization. So, I moved on to Oklahoma when a few of us decided to venture out to a group hidden there."

"Now, that one lasted longer, for about five, close to six years, and I moved up in the ranks very fast. I had at least six men joining a month and that's when I noticed the power I had over people. I decided I need to form my own group."

Stone spoke with pride in his voice. "I left there and came here. Within three years, I built what you see now. I was very pleased with the way everyone embraced my views and bonded with me so easily."

You self-centered bastard, Forbes silently raged. I'm going to get pleasure from slapping those cuffs on your wrists. "Hush isn't like other white supremacy groups. I haven't heard you mention cross-burnings or anything like that."

"No, we haven't done anything like that in the past couple of years. We're more focused on keeping our people in higher positions and making sure that the wrong kind doesn't get in. Now, if we have to do a little extra to prove our point, we will."

"Is that all that Hush does?" Forbes questioned.

Stone's eyes took on a different look at his question. "What are you talking about? Do you think that I'm involved with something else, Jacob?"

"Let's be honest with each other. I know that you aren't able to afford all this luxury with just having a few of your people in political offices. Hush has money coming in from other revenues and I want to be a part of it."

"Jacob, you seem very sure of this. Have you being looking at someone you shouldn't have?" Stone demanded.

Forbes didn't break his cover but keep moving forward. "I've worked for several powerful men as their bodyguard and by now I can spot when money is being made off drugs and weapons. Don't lie to me. As you have told me numerous times I'm the best. Why wouldn't you want the best working side by side with you for everything?"

Drumming his fingers on the dark finish of the chair's arm Stone titled his head to the side and studied him closely. "I admire how you didn't back down from me. I believe, Jacob, that you're ready for your test." Standing Stone gazed down at him. "Come with me." Turning on his heel, Stone strolled towards the door confident that Forbes would follow him.

Forbes kept following Stone until they came to a wall. He watched in stunned silence at Stone touched the center of the wall and it slid to the side. "I didn't know that was there," he uttered shocked. He had been all over this place numerous times looking of evidence to use and would have never found this place.

"You weren't supposed to know," Stone tossed back going into the hidden passage. "Keep moving, your test is waiting."

He moved behind Stone and glanced back when the door slammed shut. Where in the hell was this test going to take place? Forbes wondered as he blinked several times getting his eyes used to the dark passageway. There was an enough light to see but that was about it.

"Are you going to tell me what the test is now?"

"No, none of my other bodyguards got a warning and I'm not going to give you one either. Think of it as a pop quiz and pray you've studied enough," Stone commented stopping in front of a closed door. He nodded to a man Forbes had never seen before standing there.

"Is the test ready for Jacob?"

"Yes sir. It has been ready for a while now," the man replied. "Do you want me to stay until he finishes?"

"No, Jacob needs to do think by himself. Hand me your gun then you can leave."

"What do I need a gun for?" he questioned not liking this at all.

"Patience Jacob," Stone said taking the gun from the man handed him. "It will only be a few more minutes, then you can prove your loyalty to me."

Stone waited while the man went back then and back into the dark tunnel. "When I open this door you'll only have two minutes to take care of the problem on the other side. I want one clean shot to the head."

It took everything that Forbes had not to break his cover. Stone wanted him to kill someone in cold blood. "Who's on the other side of this door? Where did you get this person from?" He had to help this individual the best way that he could and even if it meant breaking his cover.

"Take the gun and you'll find out." Stone thrust the gun into his hand and then unlatched the door. Swinging it open, he waved at him with his right hand. "Why don't you take a look?"

The hairs on the back of his neck stood up as he got closer to the door. For some reason he had a very bad feeling about this. Something wasn't right, but he couldn't place his finger on it. Forbes stopped mere inches from the entrance and cast a glance at Stone. "Is there reason you want me to kill this person?"

"Yes, there is," Stone replied, "because I demand it of you for the family and your place at my side." The words were shouted seconds before his boss shoved him into the room and his whole world came crashing down around his feet.

"KISSA!" Forbes' horrified voice yelled spying the tied up woman lying unconscious on the floor before a blinding pain in the back of his head brought him to his knees knocking him out.

Chapter Twenty Eight

"Forbes, wake up!" Kissa shouted pulling at the tight ropes wrapped around her wrists. How in the hell did she get here? Why was Forbes passed out on the floor in front of her? She didn't know when those men would be back, but she couldn't let them find her like this. Forbes had to wake up and help her. Shaking her head she tried to clear some of the fuzziness that still lingered there.

"Forbes, wake up!" she screamed again worried now that the hard blow her kidnapper gave Forbes might have hurt him worse than she first thought.

A low moan finally slipped from his lips and it gave her the hope she had lost twenty-four hours ago. "That's it, baby. Open those killer gray eyes of yours and look at me. We need to get out of here."

Slowly Forbes eyes opened and he stared at her until realization set in. "Kissa, how did you get here?" he questioned as he tried to sit up; after a few attempts he finally made it. "Are you okay?" Forbes asked rubbing the back of his head then crawled across the floor to her. "How in the fuck did you get here?"

"I don't remember much," Kissa replied as Forbes worked on the knots securing her arms and legs. "I answered the door and there was this strange man standing there. When I asked could I help him, he sprayed something into my face, total blackness took over."

The instant she was freed his hands were all over her body, checking for bruises. "Did they touch you? Are you hurt?" Forbes asked running his fingers through her hair then pressed her face to his chest. "God, I almost had a heart attack when Stone shoved me into the room and cold cocked me before I could do anything."

Kissa leaned back so she could look into Forbes eyes. "He thought I was asleep, but I wasn't. Stone grabbed the gun off the floor and pointed it at you. I was terrified that he was going to kill you, but he didn't. He shoved the gun into the back of his pants and left. I heard the door latch behind him."

"How did he find out you were F.B.I.?" An involuntary flinch went through her body as Forbes massaged her sore wrists.

"I don't have a clue. I was always safe," he answered pressing her back to his warmth. "Are you sure that you're okay?"

"I'm as good as I could be after being kidnapped by a racist. That guy who was guarding the door kept saying horrible things about my body. I thought he might try something but he never did."

Muscular arms tightened around her frame as Forbes rested his chin on the top of her head. "I would have killed him," he grounded out the words between his teeth.

"Stop...we can't waste own energy on him. We have to find a way out of here. I know they are going to kill us, especially me. I'm not stupid. Stone hates me because I'm black and you aren't any better in his eyes for liking me."

Calloused fingers gripped Kissa's chin and her eyes connected with a pair of cool gray eyes, sparkling with love. "I'm in love with you. Repeat it."

"You're in love with me."

"Use my name."

"Agent Harrington is in love with me."

"Kissa," Forbes's voice rumbled deep in his throat. "Do it right."

"Sexy Forbes Harrington is in love with Kissa Collins," she grinned trying to forget the danger they were in.

"God...I want you so bad, but this isn't the time or place," Forbes groaned as his cock pushed against the tight material of his jeans.

"I want you too. It has been so long since we have been together," Kissa confessed. Taking Forbes' hand she slid it under the short skirt she was wearing and moaned when two hard fingers worked their way inside her damp body.

"Please..." she whimpered.

"Baby, we can't. I have to be alert to listen for someone coming back," Forbes tried to remove his hand, but she grabbed his wrist.

"I can tell you want this too." Kissa laid her hand over the thick erection dying to burst free. "Can't we just move the necessary clothes out of the way?" she asked unbuttoning his pants slipping her hand inside. The heat of him burned her hand. Wrapping her around him as much as she could Kissa stroked Forbes until he grew another inch.

"Kissa...honey we can't," Forbes grunted removing her hand and his from their bodies. He quickly buttoned up his pants and pulled down her skirt. "I swear to you that after we get out of here I'll make love to that delectable body of yours all night long."

"What if we don't make it out?" Jumping up from the floor she wrapped her arms around her waist and moved to the other side of the room. "Stone or one of his flunkies will kill us and hide the evidence."

"Don't you trust me?" Forbes' question was so low that she almost didn't hear him.

"Of course I trust you," she gasped spinning around hurt that Forbes thought so little of her. "I love you and I'm here with you until the end."

Moving until he was an inch from her, he brushed his firm lips over her softer ones. "I have a gun hidden inside the leg of my pants," he breathed into her mouth. This news blindsided her and Kissa was too startled to respond.

"Don't say a word," he whispered into her mouth again. "I'm positive the room is bugged."

"Cameras or listening devices?"

"I'm not sure, but I feel like we're being observed, don't you?" Forbes pointed out loosening his grip on her.

Kissa nodded her head. "Is that why you didn't want to make love earlier?" she questioned stepping back some.

"Yes...and I need you to do something for me."

"What is it?"

"Start a fight with me so someone will come in here and we can try to escape, but I have to make sure that you're with me. We might only get this one chance at freedom."

"I'm ready when you are." She finally trusted Forbes with her heart...why not her life?

"On the count of three..." he said softly. "One...two...three..." Forbes mouthed I love you at her then stepped back. "I can't believe you were dumb enough to let one of Stone's men bring you here. I thought you were smarter than that, but I guess I was wrong."

"How dare you!" Kissa screamed. "I was minding my own business when you came into my life with all your lies. I can't believe I slept with you. You're a worthless bastard. I hate the sight of you. Hell, I pray I get out of the mess and never have to see your face again."

"Same thing here, honey," Forbes shouted back. "When I was sleeping with you I just kept wishing it was over. I was taking one for the team because no one else at the Bureau could stomach sleeping you."

The slap hit Forbes' face before she could stop it. "You weren't the best lover in the world either." Kissa rubbed her stinging palm and raced over to the door, trying to remember that Forbes didn't mean what he was saying to her, but the last comment still hurt nevertheless.

"Let me out of here! I know someone can hear me and I want out of the damn room now. If you're going to kill me come on and do it. Stop being a coward." She slapped her palms against the steel door.

"Do you think they're going to listen to you? You aren't worth their time," Forbes taunted behind her.

"Shut up!" Kissa banged on the door some more adding in a kick or two. "I know you're out there. Open this damn door!"

Hearing the latch move, she hurriedly stepped away from the door and glanced at the man coming through the doorway. "I don't want you hear the two of you all night long. Keep quiet or I'll have to take matters into my own hands," Stone threatened. "Agent Harrington, if you love Ms. Collins, you'll keep her quiet for her own good."

"Do it. I'm sick of listening to her too," Forbes flung back.

Kissa cringed at the sexual gleam that came in Stone's eyes. "You're a very beautiful woman. It has been a very long time since I had one of you in my bed. I saw you earlier trying to seduce Jacob...I mean Forbes. Are you still wet for him? Maybe I can use that to my advantage."

"I rather die before I let your hands on my body," she retorted stepping back. "You sicken me more than Forbes."

"Oh...I want you alive and begging for me to stop." Stone's face spilt into a sickening grin as he followed her further into the room totally ignoring Forbes behind him.

"I'll never beg you for anything," Kissa taunted hoping to keep Stone's attention, so Forbes could get to the gun.

Totally caught up in his sick lust, Stone licked his lips as his eyes raked over her body striping away her clothes. "I think the first thing I'll do will be to cut those clothes from your body and tie your arms to my bed post. After that I'll spread your legs wide and lick you like you're a delicious Oreo cookie. Do you know how many of those things I can lick and eat in one night?"

"You're sick," she gasped pressing her fingers to her mouth.

"Yes...I am," Stone agreed as he lunged for her.

"Stone," Forbes shouted at them.

"What!" Stone yelled spinning back around. He didn't have time to react before the bullet hit him in the middle of his chest and he dropped dead to the floor.

Screaming, Kissa jumped over his corpse and raced over to Forbes. She tried to hug him, but he pushed her back. "We need to go now! I don't know how long we'll have to get out before his bodyguards come looking for him." Taking her by the hand, Forbes pulled her from the room and through the darkened passageway. It seemed liked they traveled for hours before they came out the other end.

Pausing in the empty living room, Forbes planted a quick kiss on her mouth and shoved her towards the front door. "Get out of here as fast as you can and make it to the highway. It's just over that hill. I'll be right behind you, but if you hear gun shots, don't look back, keep running."

"I'm not going to leave you," Kissa whispered as they made across the thick grass.

"You have to get Zane here if I can't do it. His number is 812-996-45578. It's the direct line to his phone. He'll answer it on the first ring," Forbes shouted to her as they ran for the highway. Seconds later, gun shots filled the air and a groan came from behind her.

Spinning around, Kissa saw the weapon hit the ground the second before Forbes grabbed his arm. She wasn't about to leave Forbes here to die alone on a cold, damp ground. Running back, she grabbed the gun and help Forbes up. "I told you to leave me," he snapped struggling to his feet.

"Not on your life. Now shut up and keep running. I don't know the direction the bullet came from," she said as another whizzed past her ear.

Nodding, Forbes snatched the gun out of her hand and shoved her in front of him. "Keep running and I promise that I'll be right behind you."

She took Forbes on his word and shot off in a dead run, trying to listen for his heavy steps behind her. Kissa kept running and pushed down the need to look back over her shoulder for Forbes. The long run was getting hard on her legs, but she kept at it until she spotted the highway. Pushing her body a little further, she collapsed at the edge and gasped for breath. "We made it," she whispered ecstatic that they were safe, and waited for his answer, but instead of a response she got dead silence.

Chapter Twenty Nine

"FORBES!" Kissa screamed her voice echoing through the silence that surrounded her. "Can you hear me? Please answer me." Pushing her body up off the ground, she moved back towards the trees under she heard a branch crack in the darkness. She glanced back over her shoulder debating what she should do. Forbes made her promise to get in touch with Zane, but she couldn't leave him out here all alone. Taking several deep breaths, Kissa slowly placed one foot in front of the other when a shadow stepped out from the tress.

"I thought you were dead," she cried wrapping her arms around Forbes' strong shoulders. "Why didn't you answer me when I called out to you?"

"Sweetheart, I had to lure them away from you. I wasn't about to let any of them get their hands on your sweet little body. There were only two of them and I took them out pretty quick," Forbes answered against the side of her neck.

"Thank God! I don't know what I would do if something ever happened to you. I love you so much."

Long fingers cupped her butt and yanked her closer to the erection poking her stomach, "Do you feel what your words are doing to me?"

"Is that a bad thing, agent?" Kissa mused leaning back in his arms. She never knew it felt this good to be in love with another person. Forbes was a keeper.

"Yes...damnit, when we're out in the wilderness and I don't have place to make love to you," he complained releasing her and stepping back.

"Do we have a way out of here?"

"Zane is on his way with backup. They should be here in twenty minutes."

"I don't understand," she frowned. "How were you able to get in touch with Zane?" What was going on?

Forbes pulled her back into her arms and rested his chin on her head. "One of the guys I knocked out luckily had a cell phone and I called him. I gave him all the information he needed and he's coming for us. He was stunned you were here with me."

"Lord...I know if he tells Africa, she'll be out of her mind with worry. She wanted me to get some extra time to myself, so I could think about my feelings for you. But I'm pretty sure this isn't what she had in mind."

Chuckling he ran his hands up and down Kissa's back loving the feel of her and knowing it wasn't one of his dreams. "This isn't the time or place I thought you would finally admit to your feelings for me, but I'm a greedy man so I'll take it."

"I do...." Kissa started to tell Forbes how she felt again until he covered her mouth with his hand.

"Don't say a word...I hear something," he whispered in her ear as he pushed her down into the thick grass. "Stay perfectly still until I know it's safe."

Nodding her head, Kissa bit her lip as Forbes removed his hand from her mouth and reached for the gun in the back of his pants. "If I have to start shooting I want you to stay here until I draw their fire away from you. Run in the opposite direction and you'll find help."

Kissa shook her head as tears streamed down her face. "I won't leave you."

"Yes, you will," Forbes ground out as he checked his gun for bullets. "I don't want you killed and I can't think about anything more happening to you."

She hated that Forbes was right. It wouldn't do either of them any good if they both got caught and tossed back in that room again. "Alright," Kissa agreed as the footsteps got closer.

Forbes pointed his gun in the direction the footsteps were coming from and was about to shoot when a familiar voice called out to them. "Forbes, Kissa, are you out there?" Zane whispered loudly looking around the area. "Answer me if you are. We don't have much time before the men I saw reach us."

"We're over here," Forbes answered pulling her up from their hiding position

Zane raced over to them. "Are the two of you okay? What in the hell went wrong? I had no clue Stone had kidnapped Kissa."

"I didn't know either until Stone took me to this hidden room and there she was," Forbes answered hugging Kissa to him.

"I need to fill out a report."

"I know all about procedures but I think we need to leave and quick because I hear Stone's bodyguards getting closer. It won't be long before they find the bodies of the other men."

"I agree with Forbes. I don't want to be here a moment longer. This entire place makes my skin crawl. I want to go back home and take a long hot shower," Kissa whispered running her hands up and down her bare arms.

"Well...let's go," Zane replied. "The van is just over that hill in the distance. I informed the men to wait at least an hour for us before calling reinforcements."

Turning, Forbes, Kissa, and Zane took off for the large trees in the distance. All of them sent up a silent prayer that they would be able to make it back to the van safely without anymore of Stone's guards popping up in their way.

"I can't believe we made it out of there without any problems," Kissa whispered taking another sip of the hot coffee cradled in her hands. "I thought for sure at the last second one of the men would jump out and grab me."

"I would have kill him before his hands got anywhere near you," Forbes' voice called out to her from the kitchen in his house. After taking a statement and answering all of Zane's questions, he found a way to sneak them on a plane back to Forbes' home.

"Didn't I promise that I'll always love and take care of you?" he reminded her coming back into the dining room. Taking the cup of her hands, he set it on the table and pulled her up from the chair. Sitting down, Forbes tugged her back down into his lap wrapping his arms around her waist. "I'll want to take care of you forever. You're the most important thing in my life and I wouldn't ever be able to give you up."

Kissa blinked back tears as she rested her head on Forbes' chest. "You already know how much I love you, but your job is just so dangerous. I don't know if I can be one of those girlfriends that wait by the phone not to get that one call."

"You aren't going to be one of those girlfriends, because I want you to be my wife."

Lifting her head, she stared down into a pair of perfect gray eyes. "Are you sure you still want to marry me after everything I put you though? I was really hard on you after you arrested my uncle."

"Sweetheart, you were in pain and I understand that. My shoulders are strong enough to handle those tiny blows you were throwing at them. No matter how many times your mouth told me to stay away, your eyes told me a different story and that's what I listened to."

"How about I let my body do some of the talking for a few hours?" Kissa sultry voice suggested as her fingers worked on the buttons on his shirt.

"Are you sure? We have been through a lot in the past twenty-four hours." Forbes was dying to make love to Kissa again, but he wanted to make sure she still wasn't riding an emotional roller coaster.

"Forbes, I want to be with you for the rest of my life, starting with today. Don't you believe me? Unless you're saying that you don't want me then I'll have to go and find another man who does. That one guy at the Bureau was kind of cute. I think his name was Leo."

Forbes stood up with Kissa in his arms. "Leo and any other man that looks at you crossed eyed will get their ass kicked by me. I don't share," he hissed as he carried his woman towards his bedroom.

Giggling, Kissa wrapped her arms around his neck and planted a soft kiss on his mouth. "I love that you were jealous."

"My jealousy isn't the only thing that you'll love after tonight," Forbes promised as he sauntered through his bedroom door, kicking it closed behind him.

Chapter Thirty

Brad held the envelope in his hand and tried to find the words to make her change her mind, but nothing he could think of would help. The most horrible thing that he never wanted to happen has hit him right between the eyes. Dru was leaving him. How was he supposed to come to work every day and not see her outside his door?

"No, I'm not going to accept your two weeks notice," he snapped tossing the envelope on his desk. "I don't why you ever bothered typing it out. You're meant to be here with me and this is where you're going to stay."

"Brad, you not accepting the letter won't do you any good. I'm still leaving. I feel it's for the best."

"How can you say that? I'm sorry that I got jealous of Neil. You should have told me that he was your father and I wouldn't have cared if you went to eat lunch with him."

"I'm not using Neil as an excuse either because he isn't the reason I want to find a new job...you are," Dru answered.

"I won't let you disappear out of my life. I'll come to your new job every day with flowers, candy, balloons or anything else that will win you back. Darling, I love you and don't want to lose you." Brad tossed all of his emotions out of the table for Dru to see.

"If you would just stop talking and let me get a word in," Dru sighed. "I'll tell you why I gave you my two weeks' notice."

"I don't want to hear some long speech you've memorized to let me down easily," Brad informed her.

"Why do you think always have something bad to tell you?"

"I'm not stupid. You're trying to find an easy way to get me out of your life."

"How do you expect a woman to propose to you if you don't let her speak?" Dru questioned.

"I let you talk all the time...how can you..." Brad paused in mid-sentence and stared at her. "You want to marry me?" he stuttered noticeably shock by her announcement.

"Isn't that what a proposal usually means?" she laughed leaning across the table. "Brad, I love you and I have for a very long time. I would love to have children with you and grow old together. Will you marry me?"

Brad was around the table and wrapped her in his arms in under ten seconds. "Dru, I'll marry you any day of the week, but only under one condition."

"What is the condition?"

"Let me take you out tonight and propose to you. I've been waiting for so long for that night and the look on your face."

Dru couldn't believe that Brad just asked her that. "Do you really want to redo my proposal? I thought mine was so good."

"It was beyond good...it was perfect, but I want to do a little extra."

She understood where Brad was coming from. "I'll say yes if you agree to a condition that I have." Dru grinned while her fingers played with the collar of Brad's shirt.

"You can have anything you heart desires," Brad re plied with a smile that would make any cartoon Cheshire cat jealous.

"I want to get married next week," Dru tossed out.

"Fine," Brad agreed quicker than she thought he would. "The what, when and where of the wedding doesn't matter to me. All that matters is making you my wife."

Blinking back tears, Dru realized that she almost let the best thing that had ever happened to her slip through her fingers. "I love you Brad."

"I love you too Dru and I can't wait until we begin our lives together," Brad murmured before kissing her.

Kissa held back tears as she typed the end of her latest story. She couldn't believe how fast Dru and Brad's story came together after she admitted to her feelings about Forbes. It was as if holding back from him made her story hold back from her, but everything turned out for the best after all.

"Did your couple end up with each other in the end?" Forbes asked kissing the side of her neck.

Tiny electrical currents traveled a path down her body at the slight touch of Forbes' mouth on her body. It was amazing how good it felt to finally have everything behind them. The thought of the rest of her life without Forbes shook her to the core. Anything could have happened to them out in those woods. She was given a second chance with the man she loved. She wasn't about to miss a single second of it.

"Of course, they had a happy ending. My fans wouldn't accept anything else when it came to Brad and Dru. I think they are by far my favorite couple. I hated to see them end, but it was time."

"I'll tell you something else it's time for," Forbes whispered untying the robe from around her waist pushing one side off her shoulder.

Kissa wanted to make love to Forbes again, but she couldn't until things were clear between them. Placing her hand on top of his, she shook her head. "No, we can't. I want to discuss something with you first."

"What is it?" he asked spinning her around in the seat to face him. "Are you having second thoughts about us?"

"Never...I love you more than anything in this world, but I need to be sure of something first." She debated how to start the conversation because she didn't want to upset Forbes.

"Don't let it worry you. Just tell me what it is and we'll work through it together. Isn't that what couples do?"

Nodding, Kissa said what was on her mind, "Are you leaving the F.B.I. because of me? If you are, I can't let you do it. I would feel guilty for the rest of my life. It's your life." She wasn't going to let her man give up something that he worked so hard to achieve just for her.

Pulling her out of the chair, Forbes positioned her in front of him. "I want you to listen to me and hear every word that comes out of my mouth. I was an agent for years and I loved my job, but after a while it started to bother me. I didn't find it as pleasurable as when I first joined. I was living day by day until I walked into that studio and saw you sitting behind that table."

"I knew you were a woman that I wanted to get to know better. The more I got to know you the harder it became to lie to you. I fell in love with you that day on the cover shoot, but I couldn't tell you."

"Baby, I'm leaving the Bureau because its no longer a part of me. It never was my life. A job is a thing that you do and never should be thought of as your life. I've only come across one person that I've thought about centering my life around and that is you."

"Sweetheart, I love you more than anything in this entire world and I want to spend the rest of my life making love to you, watching you grow big with our children and loving you until the day I die. I'm wishing with everything in me that you want the same thing." Forbes finished with a forlorn look that could have melted the hardest of hearts.

Kissa was at a loss for words and that was hard to acknowledge especially since she was a writer, but never in her life had anyone spoken those kinds of words to her. This was better than any scene she could have written in any of her books

"Yes...I want the same thing. I couldn't see myself with anyone else but you."

Yelling at the top of his lungs, Forbes picked her up on spun her around in a circle. "God, woman, I love you so damn much," he said placing her back on the ground. "How about we go upstairs and work on a new love scene for your next book?"

"No, I've a better idea," she said taking Forbes by the hand tugging him towards the steps. "I think we should go upstairs and work on the future, romance author to F.B.I. agent, watcha think?

"I believe the future Mrs. Forbes Huntington just found another reason for me to love her," Forbes answered as he swung Kissa in his arms and carried her back upstairs.

The End

More about Marie Rochelle:

Marie Rochelle is a bestselling author of interracial romances featuring black women and white men. Marie first started writing IR books about two years ago and it has been nonstop for her ever since. Her first best selling IR romance was entitled Taken by Storm. In addition, Marie has a very successful series called The Men of CCD and right now she's working on the much awaited third book in the series: Tempting Turner. Marie has enjoyed writing from a very young age and is happy she decided to turn her career toward the IR market; a market that she had enjoyed for years herself. She has always dreamt of being a writer and now is truly happy to see her dreams becoming a reality.

To find out more about her visit her web site: www.freewebs.com/irwriter

Red Rose Publishing:

Beneath the Surface-Available Now

Pamper Me- Available Now

Be With you

Cover Model

With all my Heart - Coming Soon

Love Play

Heat Me Up

Dangerous Bet: Troy's Revenge

Boss Man

Junk 'N Her Trunk

The William's Sister Series

<u>Cobblestone Press</u>

Special Delivery

<u>Phaze</u>

All The Fixin

My Deepest Love

A Taste of Love: Richard

Made in the USA
Lexington, KY
20 November 2009